Goddess Girls

HESTIA
THE
INVISIBLE

Goddess Girls

HESTIA
THE
INVISIBLE

JOAN HOLUB & SUZANNE WILLIAMS

Aladdin

NEW YORK   LONDON   TORONTO   SYDNEY   NEW DELHI

This book is a work of fiction. Any references to historical events, real people, or real places are used fictitiously. Other names, characters, places, and events are products of the author's imagination, and any resemblance to actual events or places or persons, living or dead, is entirely coincidental.

ALADDIN

An imprint of Simon & Schuster Children's Publishing Division

1230 Avenue of the Americas, New York, New York 10020

First Aladdin paperback edition December 2015

Text copyright © 2015 by Joan Holub and Suzanne Williams

Cover illustration copyright © 2015 by Glen Hanson

Also available in an Aladdin hardcover edition.

All rights reserved, including the right of reproduction in whole or in part in any form.

ALADDIN is a trademark of Simon & Schuster, Inc., and related logo is a registered trademark of Simon & Schuster, Inc.

For information about special discounts for bulk purchases, please contact Simon & Schuster Special Sales at 1-866-506-1949 or business@simonandschuster.com.

The Simon & Schuster Speakers Bureau can bring authors to your live event. For more information or to book an event, contact the Simon & Schuster Speakers Bureau at 1-866-248-3049 or visit our website at www.simonspeakers.com.

Book designed by Karin Paprocki

The text of this book was set in Baskerville.

Manufactured in the United States of America 1015 OFF

2 4 6 8 10 9 7 5 3 1

Library of Congress Control Number 2015933169

ISBN 978-1-4814-4999-1 (hc)

ISBN 978-1-4814-4998-4 (pbk)

ISBN 978-1-4814-5000-3 (eBook)

We appreciate our mega-incredible readers!

*Emma L., Caterina H., Jaden B., Taelyne C., Kaylee B.,
Ryanna L., Paris O., Madison W. & Kaicey E., Nevaeh H.,
Ava D., Danica P., Aubrey K., Ava C., Trena J., Elna B.,
Patrona C., Keny Y., Koko Y., Grecia V., Yasmin V., McKay O.
& Reese O., Danielle H., Ryen R., Kaitlyn G., Megan D.,
Aleese B., Riverson M., Cian B., Endreya B., Reanna C.,
Rachael C., Julia K., Gavin F., Ariel S., Jasmine R.,
Sophia O., Harper M., Caitlin R., Hannah R., Kylie S.,
Anh H., the Andraue Family & Alba C., Micci S. & Brianna I.,
Shelby Lynn J. & Virginia Anna J., Lily Ann S. & Marnie S.,
Trinity N., Valerie B. & Donna B., Kaitlyn W., Maryam Y.
& Noor Y., Ava K., Subira J., Lisa A. & Peyton A., Kasidy Y.,
Jamie E.S., Corey H., Emily G., Niki K., Anna K., Keira J.,
Amanda W., Christine D.-H. & Khanya S., Sharry G., Sophie G.
& Jessica G., Lillia L., Paola F. & Andrea F., Lorelai M., Cassie G.,
Sam R., Aspasia K., Kara F., Tess S., Lana W., Jenny G.,
Emma J., Sofia W., Samantha S., Camille C., Vivian Z.,
Mackenzie S., Rachel B., Sabrina C., Keyra M., Lori F.,
Rohan T., and you!
—J.H. & S.W.*

CONTENTS

Prologue

Four years before our story begins

CAN WE BORROW SOME FIRE?" A WOMAN ASKED Hestia's mother. "Your family always seems to have it. But our fire has gone out, and I need to cook a stew for lunch."

Eight-year-old Hestia and her m...

ing the central square of thei...

outdoor public gatherin...

shopping day, and ve...

had all come to the...

Hestia's shoulders drooped as her mom now turned back toward home after assuring the woman she could certainly have some of the fire from their hearth. It wasn't fair! Her mom had promised to show her how to make an apple pie if they could find fresh fruit today. But now they'd have to trudge back home and set a piece of kindling wood ablaze from the fire Hestia had lit in their family's hearth an hour before.

Creating fire was Hestia's special skill. However, her parents had told her to keep this ability a secret. They'd feared their neighbors might not understand it. Hestia wasn't thinking of her parents' warning right now, though. She only knew that by the time they got back to this square, the food vendors would be sold out of apples.

"___ait!" Hestia called. Her mom and the other ___ after her in surprise as she ran to the center of the village square. Bending, Hestia gathered a few sticks lying nearby and piled them together. Cupping her hands, she murmured secret words in a low voice. Instantly, a small flame flared between her palms. She touched it to the kindling, setting it alight.

"There," Hestia said, smiling in satisfaction. She stood back from the blazing fire to look at the two women who had followed her. Then she had a little brainstorm. "Why not keep feeding this fire so it will burn here in the public square all the time?" she suggested. "That way, everyone can borrow fire from it whenever they want." And they wouldn't have to interrupt her family all the time to borrow fire from their hearth! "She made fire!" someone shouted nearby.

Hestia turned then, and was astonished to see

that a crowd of villagers had gathered around her. There were murmurs and gasps. And what seemed like hundreds of curious eyes, all aimed her way. The villagers said things like:

"Her idea for a public hearth is great!"

"Yeah, instead of each trying to light our own fires every day, it would mean we could come borrow fire here anytime we need it."

"So we'll never run out of fire!"

Hestia moved to her mom's side and slipped her small fingers into her mothers' hand, hiding shyly behind her mom's skirts. She wasn't used to such attention. "Can we go get the apples now, Mom?" she whispered.

She had no idea that what had seemed like a simple act to her was about to change her whole life.

The very next day Hestia was called to attend

third grade at Mount Olympus Academy. She was an immortal it seemed, and was officially given the title "goddessgirl of the hearth." She was on her way to meet Zeus himself, the King of the Gods and Ruler of the Heavens!

1

Symbols

Four years later

"TODAY WE WILL TAKE A BREAK FROM POTTERY design and painting," announced Mr. Phintias on Friday at the start of second-period Crafts-ology. He was standing in front of a wall of shelves lined with vases, urns, and pots. Many were decorated with reddish-orange silhouette figures on glazed black backgrounds. The amazing feats of the gods and goddesses of Mount Olympus were the main subjects of these painted scenes. And this teacher had created much of the stunningly beautiful clay pottery himself!

At his announcement most of the class groaned with disappointment. Reluctantly they started putting away the clay they'd begun unwrapping, as well as their sculpting tools and paintbrushes.

However, twelve-year-old Hestia breathed a sigh of relief as she plunked her half-finished clay pot back onto its shelf. While other students had unique, fantastical, or elegant pots, bowls, and urns in progress, her pot was plain old boring in her opinion. The kind you could buy anywhere down on Earth.

Hearing the groans, Mr. Phintias ran a hand over his short brown ponytail. "Hey, no worries. We'll return to pottery soon enough. But today we're going to investigate a new artistic skill."

He was one of Mount Olympus Academy's most mega-cool teachers, far younger and hipper than some teachers, such as Mr. Cyclops, who taught Hero-ology. However, making painted pottery was Mr. Phintias's life. And he didn't always understand that not everyone was necessarily as excited about it. At least Hestia wasn't. The craft of pottery-making was just not her thing.

As she sat back down at her table, her fingers reached into the pocket of the tomato-red chiton she wore. They touched the edges of the blank cards she always carried, just in case she had a recipe brainstorm and wanted to jot down ideas and ingredients. She'd much rather use her creativity to come up with tasty concoctions to fill those pretty pots, bowls, and urns they made in this class. In other words, *her* favorite art was cooking!

What the teacher said next brought curious stares. "Today we will dip our feather pens into the exciting world of graphic design. As you know, mortals down on Earth will be voting one week from today to honor the MOA student they feel most deserves recognition for his or her service to humankind."

He paused as a murmur of voices indicated that students were indeed aware of the Service to Humankind contest. As they quieted, his dark brown eyes swept the room, flicking from student to student. Hestia quickly repositioned herself behind a mortal girl named Pandora at her table. Fingers crossed Hestia wouldn't be called on for anything.

"Are you deserving of such recognition?" Mr. Phintias asked the class. "Have you done something to help make the world a better, happier place for humankind? I hope so, since it's the right thing to do.

However, this is something you must judge for yourself. And if you believe the answer to this question is yes, then I strongly suggest you sign up to enter. The award will be well worth winning—"

"What is the award, exactly?" Pandora interrupted.

"That will be revealed at a banquet in honor of the eleven finalists, when one of them is announced the winner," the teacher replied with a small smile in Pandora's direction.

The violet-eyed godboy Dionysus shook a lock of curly brown hair from his forehead and gave the muscular boy sitting next to him a friendly fist thump on the shoulder. "If ridding the world of man-eating lions, arrow-shooting birds, and other dastardly creatures counts as service, then this guy is a shoo-in for the award."

The student he'd thumped was Heracles, a

superstrong mortal who wore a lion-skin cape with jaws that fit over his head like a helmet. That monstrous lion had once terrorized an entire village till Heracles had fought it and won.

"Aw, thanks, god-dude," Heracles replied humbly. He gave his enormous knobby club, which was leaning up against the table beside him, a spin. "Though, I gotta say," he added, "ridding King Augeas's stable of poop was way worse than any of those other labors!"

"Eew," squealed a couple of girls, making ick faces. But Hestia and the rest of the class laughed. Heracles had done all those things (and more) as part of twelve labors he'd performed in order to win a permanent place as a student at the Academy.

Their illustrious school was perched at the very top of Mount Olympus, the highest mountain in Greece. Mostly godboys and goddessgirls went here, but Principal Zeus had also invited a handful of mortals, like Heracles, to attend.

With a tolerant smile Mr. Phintias went on, his tone taking on a proud note. "I and three other artists have been accorded the honor of painting a large mural in Principal Zeus's temple at Olympia, where voting for the award will take place. This mural will take up most of one wall. It will be painted in a jeweled palette of terra-cottas, ceruleans, and . . ."

For a few minutes, he happily described in way more detail than was necessary the art techniques and materials he and the other artists would use. As his dark eyes twinkled and he gestured broadly, Hestia realized that the prospect of painting the mural was as exciting to him as creating a new recipe and trying it out in the school's kitchen was to her. In a way, they were both artists! Clay and paint were his raw materials. Hers were spices, flour, and other foodstuffs.

After a while the teacher seemed to come back down to Earth—or to MOA, anyway. "Ahem, returning to the subject at hand," he went on. "The subject of the mural in Olympia will be images of the eleven finalists selected by the awards committee. The images will remind mortals who visit the temple of their choices for voting."

As he began walking around the room and through the spaces between the tables where students sat, heads turned to follow the teacher. "So, you are likely wondering what all this has to do with today's Craftsology assignment. Well, graphic design is a fascinating, specialized skill that can encompass the design of scrollazines, books, shields, product packaging, logos, and much more. And what I would like each of you to do this morning is to come up with your own logo—a *symbol*, that is—to represent your highest, most exalted self." He grinned and winked at them.

"You mean like my symbol might be a lion?" Heracles piped up.

"You got it," said Mr. Phintias, nodding. Then to the class he added, "Your choices should reflect how you want worshipful mortals on Earth to think of you. You'll want to pick a symbol that best represents how you've helped humankind, as Heracles has done. If you're a finalist for the award, your image will hold this symbol in the mural we'll paint. Even if you're not yet sure you'll enter the contest, this assignment is still part of your grade for this class, so let's get cracking, shall we?"

Now the teacher passed around blank sheets of papyrus for them to sketch ideas on. "I'll give you fifteen minutes to come up with possible logos, and then we'll share them in class. Try to choose something with power and pizzazz. Your aim with this symbol is to impress mortals. For example, if Principal Zeus were to do this assignment, he might choose a ferocious and crackling thunderbolt of the kind he uses against enemies in battle."

"Oh, I get it," Pandora said. "This symbol-logo thing is like our brand? I mean, Zeus is known for hurling thunderbolts, right? Like, how there's a thunderbolt on the wax seal he stamps on letters? And how he puts thunderbolts on the sides of the school chariots, too? And—"

"Exactly," Mr. Phintias said, gently cutting her off. Because if he hadn't, her questions would likely have multiplied so fast, they'd have taken up the rest of class time!

Famed for her curiosity, Pandora often spoke in

questions even when making statements. *Her symbol or logo should definitely be a question mark,* thought Hestia. But wait. Pandora was already using that logo, come to think of it. She wore her bangs in the shape of question marks. Hestia had even seen her in the hallway of MOA's fourth-floor girls' dorm wearing pj's decorated with question marks. So this assignment should be an easy-peasy one for her!

Must be nice, thought Hestia as she stared down at the fresh sheet of papyrus Mr. Phintias had placed before her. Because suddenly her mind had gone as blank as the papyrus was.

What should my symbol be? she wondered. *What should I choose?* She brushed the fluffy end of her self-inking feather pen against her cheek. Knowing she only had minutes to come up with a logo, familiar feelings of panic welled up inside. She'd never been good at in-class assignments. She didn't like being put on the spot like this. Why couldn't the task of coming up with a logo have been homework, so she could've had more time to think?

She glanced around the room. The others all seemed to be busily sketching. *Gulp.*

Of course, the student who probably had the best shot at winning this Service to Humankind Award wasn't even in this class: Principal Zeus's daughter, Athena. That brainy girl's numerous inventions had helped mortals a lot.

She had invented sailing ships, musical instruments like the flute and the trumpet, weaving and other needle arts, and the plow (which made it easier for farmers to plant rows in their fields). Then there was the olive, which had many uses. Its oil burned brightly in lamps. It was a popular food, too, and olive wood was good for building homes. Athena had already helped humans so much that they'd named the city of Athens after her!

Hestia pushed the tip of her feather pen across the paper, trying to look as busy as everyone else seemed to be. Really, she was only making doodles. She drew a little owl—one of Athena's symbols—that turned out to accidentally resemble a cat.

If that goddessgirl entered the contest, her only problem with this assignment would be the hard time she'd have choosing between many possible symbols. One of her titles was the goddess of wisdom. Sometimes she wore owl earrings or other jewelry with wise owl designs. Hestia really admired the girl. Along with her BFFs—Aphrodite, Persephone, and Artemis—Athena was one of the most popular goddessgirls at MOA.

"What do you think of this?" she overheard another girl say from the table right next to her own. It was Aphrodite, the goddessgirl of love and beauty. She was holding up a sketch of a bouquet of red and pink hearts to show Pandora.

"Nice," Pandora replied. "Your Lonely Hearts Club has helped tons of mortals find love. Is that why you chose that logo? I bet you'll get their votes for sure!"

"Think so?" said the beautiful Aphrodite, sounding pleased.

Hestia watched the goddessgirl push her long golden hair, which was threaded with pink satin ribbons, behind her perfectly shaped ears. Then Aphrodite reached for a glittery pink handbag that was hanging on the back of her chair and took out a tube of lip gloss.

The color of the bag perfectly matched the chiton

she wore. Her handbag and the chiton were probably new, since Hestia had never seen them before. How many purses and chitons did that goddessgirl have, anyway? A mega-zillion? And she looked fabulous with all of them!

Hestia admired Aphrodite almost as much as she did Athena, despite the fact that Hestia and the goddessgirl of love and beauty were practically total opposites. Aphrodite was as outgoing and fashionable as Hestia was shy and clueless about fashion.

The beautiful goddessgirl's Lonely Hearts Club really had helped many mortals find happiness. Why, she'd even helped Principal Zeus find true love with the goddess Hera, who was now his wife! Hmm. Pandora could be right. Mortals did like finding love. Maybe Aphrodite would win this award.

Looking around the room, Hestia noticed that almost everyone had already sketched at least one idea for a symbol. And all the ones she could see seemed more awesome than anything she could come up with for herself. Heracles had drawn a lion's head. Dionysus had drawn masks of comedy and tragedy. As the male lead in almost all the school plays, his acting had inspired hundreds of mortal playwrights, poets, and actors.

And Iris, the goddessgirl of rainbows, had helped save the world from the rampages of a terrible Titan monster named Typhon. So she had drawn—what else?—a colorful and sparkly rainbow such as the one she'd traveled across during her adventures. Talk about pizzazz!

When Hestia saw Mr. Phintias glance at the sundial outside the classroom window, she knew time was running out. "One more minute," he announced.

A new bolt of panic shot through her like one of Zeus's thunderbolts. In the nick of time she scribbled the first thing that came to mind.

"All right," the teacher said just as she finally sketched an idea. "Who would like to share first?"

Hands instantly waved in the air. But Hestia, true to her shy nature, did her best to become invisible. Ducking her head, she let her light-brown curls fall across her cheeks. She closed herself up like a turtle, pulling the red hood she wore forward to shadow her face. She'd added hoods to the pattern she used to make all of her home-sewn chitons. They were perfect for hiding out in. And cute, too!

This attention-avoiding strategy had worked surprisingly well for her in the four years she'd been at MOA. Especially since there was never any shortage of other, more eager-to-talk students for teachers to pick from.

Her invisibility strategy might have worked today too, if she hadn't blown her cover. It was nearly the end of the period when muscle-bound Atlas, MOA's champion weight lifter, held up his symbol. He'd drawn two horizontal parallel lines, except the top line had a bump in the middle. Everyone squinted at it.

"Is it a hill beside a road?" Pandora asked.

"Or a snake who's swallowed a mouse?" Dionysus guessed.

Atlas frowned. "No and no," he said, sounding frustrated. "Can't you tell?" He held the picture out toward them.

Hestia felt sorry for him. The poor guy was an even worse artist than she considered herself to be!

But still, knowing that Atlas's great claim to fame was his strength, she could guess what he'd been trying to draw. When no one else spoke up, she summoned enough courage to blurt out, "It's a muscled arm."

Atlas beamed at her. "Right! *Muscles.* Because of the time I held up the sky so that it wouldn't fall on mortals and crush them. And skies are not exactly lightweight, ya know."

No one contradicted his version of that event, even though most of them knew that "holding up the sky" had only been a joke Heracles had played on the big guy. The sky couldn't really fall down, after all. Atlas might have been mega-strong, but he wasn't the sharpest knife in the drawer. Still, no one wanted to hurt his feelings with the truth, so they all played along.

Because there were only a few minutes left in the period, Hestia had begun to relax. She'd figured she was off the hook for sharing. Unfortunately, her blurt-out had drawn Mr. Phintias's attention. His eyes fastened on her as Atlas retook his seat. Her clasped hands tightened as she sat there, dreading what she knew in her heart was coming.

And then her teacher did in fact do the unthinkable. "Hestia," he said, "would you please share your symbol with the class?"

Hestia froze in her chair. Her mouth went dry. "I . . . um . . . I . . . " she mumbled softly.

"Huh?" "What did she say?" students murmured. They cupped their ears and strained toward her.

"Give her a second," advised a godboy named Ascalabus (Asca for short) who sat one table over. He had black hair with a natural green stripe through it that matched his lizard tail.

All the attention only made Hestia tug her hood

farther over her face and slide lower in her seat in embarrassment.

"Please stand and speak out. That way we can all hear you," Mr. Phintias told her. His voice was firm but not unkind.

Wishing she could sink into the floor, Hestia nevertheless did as instructed. She got to her feet. She hoped the end-of-class lyrebell would ring before she could speak, but no such luck.

Slowly, she held up her drawing of what looked like a big bowl with a lid and a semicircular handle on top. "It's a . . . a kettle."

A ripple of surprised laughter ran through the classroom. "You mean like a cooking pot?" Pandora asked, peering closely at Hestia's drawing.

Hestia flushed deeply. Mortified, she nodded. What was wrong with her choice of symbol? Cooking was what she liked to do, and it was also what she was best at. She usually didn't try anything too exotic but mostly stuck to plain, hearty fare using simple tools—like a kettle. Admittedly, however, not many students knew she liked to cook. She'd always been way too shy to share her enthusiasm with them. So their current confusion was sort of understandable.

"It's a fitting symbol since you're goddessgirl of the hearth," Mr. Phintias said gently. "But do you think it has enough pizzazz? Remember, the symbol you choose will influence how mortals see you. You don't want to appear too humble."

"Okay. I'll . . . um . . . think about it some more," Hestia mumbled, taking her seat again in relief.

Ping. Ping. Ping. At long last the lyrebell chimed.

As students began to gather up their belongings, Mr. Phintias called out, "The Service to Humankind

Award sign-up sheet will be posted near the lockers first thing Monday morning. That will give you the weekend to think about your symbols, which you'll need to note when you sign up."

Hestia crumpled her sketch and shoved it into her schoolbag. Still stinging from the class's reaction to her kettle symbol, she left the room as quickly as possible. Keeping her hooded head down and avoiding eye contact with anyone, she managed to ward off conversation. It didn't matter what symbol she chose. No way would she enter the contest. Who wanted a bunch of people staring at their image in a giant mural? Not her!

On her way down the hall, she stopped near the lockers to take a drink from a golden fountain along the wall. Instead of spouting water, the fountains at the Academy spouted nectar.

Hestia drank deeply. The cool nectar soothed her some after what had just happened. And because she was an immortal, it made her skin glow more brightly. (Nectar had no effect on the few mortals who also attended the Academy, however.)

As students passed behind her, she heard someone say, "A hearth is the floor of a fireplace, right?"

Hestia peeked over her shoulder. It was Aphrodite speaking with her friend Persephone, the goddessgirl of spring and growing plants. They had stopped to pull textscrolls from their lockers. With all the activity in the hall, Hestia couldn't quite catch what else Aphrodite said. However, she did catch the words "ordinary kettle" and "fits her personality."

Did that mean Aphrodite thought she was as ordinary as a cooking pot? Ears burning, Hestia was suddenly glad for the "invisibility" her hood provided.

The two goddessgirls never glanced her way, and a moment later they moved off.

Maybe I am ordinary, thought Hestia. *So what?* Still, that remark of Aphrodite's had kind of hurt. Everyone wanted to be special in some way. Even ordinary old her. She'd always admired Aphrodite, who was so beautiful that boys couldn't help staring at her. Hestia wouldn't want that for herself, of course. She didn't like to be stared at. But being practically invisible wasn't so great either. Somewhere in between might be better. Just normal recognition.

As she headed for the cafeteria, where she apprenticed in the kitchen during third period, a desire to make a change slowly kindled in Hestia like a fire starting in a hearth.

2

Kitchen Fun

HESTIA THREADED HER WAY THROUGH THE empty tables and chairs that filled the MOA cafeteria. It was quiet now, but after third period ended it would quickly become noisy and full of hungry students. At the far end she swung through the kitchen door and went straight to the fireplace hearth, as usual.

Her brown-eyed gaze fell on the sticks of wood stacked under a big, black kettle that was partly filled with water. This was the very pot she'd drawn in Crafts-ology class for her symbol. The ordinary pot that Aphrodite thought was a perfect fit for her personality. Whatever!

Stooping a little, Hestia chanted a quick spell—one she'd made up herself.

"Come, spark,

Light the dark.

Blaze higher,

Make a fire."

Instantly, a tiny yellow flame leaped between the sticks. Hestia spread her arms wide, causing the flame to blaze higher with oranges and reds. Oops! Maybe that was too big a fire. She brought her arms closer together, and the blaze lowered as a result. In seconds she'd created a crackling fire that was just the right size for cooking.

Ms. Okto, the head cafeteria lady, was working over at the butcher-block counter. Her eight octopus-like arms were busily chopping multiple vegetables. Noticing the flame, she paused to compliment Hestia. "Nice job, peanut. I've never known anyone who could get a perfect fire going as quickly as you can." She was always calling people by food nicknames and sprinkling her speech with food-related sayings.

"Thanks," said Hestia, going over to wash her hands at the kitchen sink. As far as she knew, none of the students at MOA were aware of her ability to create fire. Which was fine with her, she thought, as she straightened up from the sink. She was no show-off. Besides, compared to the talents of others at the Academy, such as Aphrodite's matchmaking skills, Heracles' strength, or Athena's fabulous olive invention, her flame talent burned low. Speaking of olives . . .

"Hey, I'm thinking of making olive bread. Okay?" she asked Ms. Okto.

The head cafeteria lady paused mid-chop again. "Your call, pumpkin. Students love everything you make." Ms. Okto had filled a pot with water and was now hanging it over the newly made fire.

Smiling at her kind words, Hestia went over to the bowl of bread dough resting on one of the large wooden kitchen counters. She'd mixed it up before breakfast that morning. By now the dough had risen above the bowl and doubled in size. After removing the cloth covering it, she punched down the dough with a fist. It was soothing work, and some of the troubles that had followed her from her last class began to fall away.

Thunk! Thunk! Clink! Ms. Okto's eight arms were a blur as she got to work again, simultaneously chopping and dumping the veggies she'd cut up into a bowl to begin a humongous salad.

After adding pitted olives to the dough, Hestia began to knead it a second time. Hmm. This bread could use some . . . pizzazz, she concluded, as Mr. Phintias's word from Crafts-ology class popped into her mind. Was she up for something bold and a teeny bit risky, cooking-wise? She was!

She tossed a handful of an herb called rosemary into the dough. Normally, she stuck to simple spices like salt and pepper, but she had a hunch that the rosemary might go well with the olives. She hoped she was right, because nobody needed a bunch of students unhappy with the food at lunchtime.

Humming a little tune, she pushed down on the dough with the heels of her hands and folded it over and over again. After dividing the bread dough into six parts, Hestia patted each lump into a big round loaf and set the loaves on trays to rise again. She never tired of the many little tasks involved in cooking. Working in MOA's kitchen felt as natural to her as . . . well . . . as swimming in the sea must feel to MOA's newest student, a mermaid named Amphitrite.

Ms. Okto picked up the huge bowl of veggies. "Could you start the yambrosia while I take this salad out to the serving area?"

"Sure," Hestia agreed. Many of the dishes served regularly in the cafeteria—like yambrosia stew, celestial salad, and nectaroni—were recipes Hestia had developed in the years she'd been at MOA. She'd taken great pleasure in naming those dishes as well. Because a good name added to a dish's appeal!

She gathered chunks of yam Ms. Okto had cut and as many of the other chopped veggies as would fit into a big bowl, and headed for the kettle over the fire. Meanwhile, Ms. Okto headed out the kitchen door to the serving area. It was time to start setting things up for lunch, which would be served after the end of this period.

As Ms. Okto left, she nodded to a second cafeteria lady entering the kitchen through the door. This one had a long snout like an anteater. She was holding a tray and sucking up crumbs of leftover food on it.

Though Hestia had often seen the snouty lunch lady doing this, the sight still startled her momentarily. The bowl she was carrying tipped, and a piece of yam rolled across the floor.

"Got it!" the lunch lady crowed happily. She tossed the tray into the sink and rushed over to neatly vacuum up the yam chunk with her long snout. "Mmm. Tasty!" she declared, raising and lowering her eyebrows in a silly way.

Hestia grinned back as she dumped the contents of her bowl into the kettle. "Thanks, Ms. Xena." The cleanliness of the cafeteria and the kitchen was largely due to this snouty lunch lady. Ms. Xena (who had shortened her name from Ms. Xenarthra to make it easier to pronounce) could suck up crumbs and pieces of food from the floor or tables lightning-fast. This talent really came in handy during cleanup.

"No problem. I *yam* a big fan of yams," Ms. Xena joked.

Hestia laughed. Of all the lunch ladies, Ms. Xena was her favorite. Ms. Xena had pretty much rescued her from loneliness when Hestia had started school at MOA back in third grade.

After noticing her hanging around the kitchen after meals, Ms. Xena had started giving her small tasks to do. At first it had been stuff like peeling vegetables and testing cookie batters. Slowly, Hestia had proved herself capable of much more, and by now she had become a trusted member of the kitchen staff.

Straightening from the kettle, Hestia went to fetch some chicken broth from the larder, which was a small closet cooled by blocks of ice. Earlier this year Ms. Xena and Ms. Okto had somehow squared it with Ms. Hydra (Principal Zeus's administrative assistant) so Hestia could apprentice as a cook this period every day. This opportunity meant the world to Hestia, making her feel needed, appreciated, and much more a part of MOA. It had pretty much changed her life. For the better.

Back from the larder, Hestia added some broth to the water and vegetables already in the kettle.

"Mmm," said Ms. Xena, snout-sniffing the air. "Is that yambrosia I smell?"

"Mm-hmm," Hestia told her as she went to fetch a

big wooden spoon for stirring. "Your snout is never wrong. I just need to add a few more veggies."

"I'll do it," Ms. Xena said eagerly. She scooped up the remaining veggies Ms. Okto had chopped and tossed them into the cooking pot hanging over the fire. She accidentally-on-purpose dropped a few, just so she could suck them up. "I'll lee the spy oh you, tho," she mumbled.

Hestia knew Mrs. Xena well enough by now to easily translate that veggie-eating-speak into: "I'll leave the spices to you, though."

"Okay," Hestia agreed, hiding a grin.

The last time Ms. Xena had spiced the yambrosia, she'd added so much pepper that it had practically set the throats of the students who ate it on fire! Though an expert at food preparation tasks like chopping, slicing, and dicing, Ms. Xena didn't have Ms. Okto's

41

and Hestia's flair for making up recipes and judging the balance of ingredients.

Ms. Xena moved to the sink to wash dishes as Hestia returned with the big wooden spoon, and the salt and pepper, too. Bending over the cooking pot, she stirred and did tastings after each addition of the seasonings. The big, black kettle reminded her of how students in her Crafts-ology class had laughed when she'd picked it as her symbol for the Service to Humankind contest.

She was telling Ms. Xena what had happened when Ms. Okto returned and overheard.

"Who gives a fig what they think?" Ms. Okto huffed.

"Right!" Looking annoyed, Ms. Xena took the pan she'd been cleaning and whacked it against the countertop. "If any of them ever had to miss a few hot meals, they might think more highly of the power of the kettle."

"Good point," said Hestia. These cafeteria ladies were often wise, as well as kind. And if she was feeling down, talking to them never failed to lift her spirits. They continued talking about this and that as they worked companionably together to prepare the rest of the meal.

Hestia had just slid the six loaves of rosemary-olive bread into the baking oven when *Bam!* The kitchen door swung open, hitting the wall. Out of the blue, Principal Zeus had arrived! (Sometimes he didn't know his own strength.)

"You there, Ms. Okto!" he thundered. "We need to talk!"

Despite the fact that he wasn't addressing her, Hestia shrank back against the nearest countertop. She'd never actually spoken to Zeus in the entire time she'd been at MOA. He'd been away on an emergency her first day of third grade and thus had been unable to welcome her. Somehow that missed meeting had never been made up, and she sometimes wondered if he even knew who she was!

Seeing as how he was seven feet tall, with bulging muscles, piercing blue eyes, and wild red hair, it was no wonder she found him intimidating. And truthfully, so did a lot of other students.

But Ms. Okto was unflappable. "What can I do for you?" she asked him calmly, wiping all eight of her hands on her apron.

"I need to order some food. *Lots* of food," Zeus said. The wide, flat golden bracelets encircling his wrists flashed in the late-morning light streaming in through the kitchen window as he made circles in the air to indicate great heaps. "For a banquet one week from tomorrow—Saturday."

Ms. Okto nodded and grabbed a feather pen and a notescroll. "Sounds like we'll be as busy as popcorn on a skillet! How many in attendance? What's the theme of the gathering?"

Just then, another man stepped forward from behind Zeus. He was wearing a tall white hat and a starched white apron. "I believe that is my purview," the man said snootily. "Permit me to introduce myself. Chef Soterides, personal cook for King Nikomedes in the country of Bithynia." He executed a curt bow.

Hearing this, Ms. Xena's mouth dropped open. She stared at the chef in awe.

But Ms. Okto seemed unimpressed. "Too many cooks spoil the broth. Especially *certain* cooks," she muttered. Did she know him? Hestia wondered. In any case she seemed to dislike Chef Soterides. But Zeus didn't appear to notice.

He, the chef, and Ms. Okto began discussing the number of guests. Then Zeus added, "The banquet is to honor the finalists and the winner of the Service to Humankind Award and . . ."

His words tapered off. He lifted his face and sniffed the air. "What is that scrumptious smell?"

Um, food? Hestia wanted to reply. *This is a kitchen, after all.* But she didn't say that aloud.

"It's some kind of spice . . . ," Zeus went on, his expression both thoughtful and blissful. He was on the move now, following his nose and searching for the source.

Meanwhile, Ms. Okto and the new chef were bent over the counter, discussing something in low murmurs. If you could call it a discussion. They actually seemed to be arguing.

By now Zeus was sniffing around the ovens. "Aha! I've found it. Something baking in the oven."

"Rosemary and olives," Ms. Okto informed him, gesturing in Hestia's direction with her pen. "Hestia's idea to add them to the bread today."

When Zeus momentarily glanced in her direction, Hestia gasped inwardly and quickly turned away. Grabbing a cloth lying on the counter, she pretended to wipe down the already clean countertop.

Did he wonder why a student was in the kitchen? Would he think she was required to be here? That she was being punished with cleanup duty for breaking school rules? Ms. Hydra had approved her cooking apprenticeship, of course, but that didn't necessarily mean that Zeus knew about it.

But if he wondered why Hestia was there, Zeus was far too entranced by the smell of the baking bread to ask.

"That bread needs to bake a while longer. How

about if I send a loaf up to your office later?" offered Ms. Okto. Zeus appeared a little disappointed about the wait, but he nodded.

Hestia kind of wished Ms. Okto hadn't made that offer. What if the bread only smelled good but tasted ooky? Could happen. She was a good cook, but she wasn't perfect. A few seconds later Zeus and the chef departed the kitchen.

Coward, Hestia scolded herself after they'd gone. She should have spoken up when Zeus had looked at her, instead of turning away. She caught a glimpse of her face in the oven's glass. Did she always look this meek? What must Principal Zeus and that chef have thought of her?

Just as it happened earlier, the desire to make changes—to somehow improve herself and her life here at MOA—flamed up in her again. A determined expression crossed her reflected face.

The minute the men were gone, Ms. Xena dug out an old issue of *Teen Scrollazine* from a drawer and brought it to show Ms. Okto and Hestia. Despite the name, the 'zine was mega-popular with young and old, immortals and mortals alike. "Look at this. That chef is famous!" Ms. Xena crowed. She pointed to a drawing of the man Zeus had brought, which accompanied a full-page article about him.

"Hmph! Stuck-up, too," Ms. Okto huffed, hardly sparing the scroll a glance. "I hope he doesn't expect me to walk on eggshells around him. We've handled many a banquet on our own. We even supplied the food for those Temple Games that Zeus held recently. So why does he suddenly think we require help?"

"Zeus is the big cheese around here, so what are you going to do?" said Ms. Xena, slipping in a metaphor that Ms. Okto might have come up with herself.

"Put on the best banquet ever?" suggested Hestia.

"Exactly!" said Ms. Okto, pointing a wooden spoon at her. "In spite of Chef Big-Britches Anchovy."

Hestia and Ms. Xena exchanged looks. *What was that nickname was all about?* their expressions conveyed. But wisely they steered talk away from the subject of the chef for now.

"Count me in to help," Hestia promised.

"And me," declared Ms. Xena.

"All for one and one for all," said Ms. Okto. The three of them high-fived. Then the two ladies left to finalize things in the cafeteria serving area, since it would soon be lunch.

Once the door swung shut behind them, Hestia whipped out one of the blank cards from the pocket of her chiton. Zeus's visit had given her an idea for a recipe. Not the food kind. No, it was a recipe to cook up a new *her*! Or to make improvements, anyway.

Quickly, she jotted down five simple things she'd always wanted to do but had never had the guts to:

1. SIT WITH SOMEONE NEW AT LUNCH.

2. STAND UP FOR SOMEONE.

3. TALK TO A BOY.

4. TRY SOMETHING I'D NORMALLY SAY NO TO.

5. TAKE A TRULY BIG, BOLD COOKING RISK!

As the lyrebell chimed to signal the end of third period and the beginning of lunch, she quickly shoved her recipe for change into her pocket.

Would she manage to accomplish all five tasks? Hestia wondered. As Ms. Okto might say, she could only hope doing so would turn out to be as easy as pie.

3

Cafeteria Blues

IF IT WERE UP TO HESTIA, SHE'D EAT ALL HER meals in the kitchen. However, just after she'd taken the delicious-smelling loaves of bread out of the oven and set them on the counter to cool, Ms. Xena came in and shooed her out as usual. "As much as we love your company, you also need to hang out with friends your own age," she told Hestia. She'd told her that same thing on more than one occasion.

Hestia reluctantly departed the kitchen and went out into the main cafeteria, which was quickly filling with students. *Argh!* Adults just didn't get it sometimes, she thought as she picked up a tray and joined the end of the lunch line. Just thinking about where she was going to sit in this cafeteria and who she might sit with was already making her feel anxious.

Holding her empty tray under one arm, she pulled her hood down a little with her opposite hand, just enough so it shadowed her face. But not so far that it looked creepy or anything. Then she shuffled a few steps closer to the lunch counter as the line moved up.

The godboy Kydoimos and his buddy Makhai were just ahead of her, joking around with each other. By now voices and laughter rang throughout the cafeteria. Her gaze scanned the room for an empty seat she could shoot for once she got her lunch. She halfway considered getting out of line and going to the back of it to start over again. It would give her something to do and use up some time. Maybe make her seem busy instead of friendless and pathetic.

When she'd first come to MOA, she had searched her pale pink *Goddessgirl Guide* scroll for advice on making friends. But there was no chapter on that. Too bad there wasn't a *Friendship Guide* scroll she could consult to answer her most perplexing questions.

Like, how many times do you need to talk to someone to call them a friend? Five times? Ten? Twenty? A hundred? That was a lot of talking for someone as shy as she was. And maybe it wasn't enough just to talk. Maybe you had to do stuff together too. Like going to get shakes at the Supernatural Market. Or shopping together at the Immortal Marketplace. She'd done these things before, but usually by herself. Because she'd always been too shy to ask anyone along. What if they said no? She'd be crushed!

By now Hestia was just a few steps from the lunch counter. Close enough to see Ms. Okto and Ms. Xena serving up today's menu of celestial salad, yambrosia stew, and . . . rosemary-olive bread? One of the lunch ladies must have returned to the kitchen for it shortly after Hestia had left to go stand in line. They must have decided it wasn't too hot to serve. She really wished she'd had a chance to taste the results of her new recipe first. Too late for that now, though.

Ahead of her, Kydoimos held out his tray to Ms. Xena. He and Makhai had earned a certain reputation at MOA. Unfortunately, it wasn't a good one. They were the two godboys most often punished with cafeteria cleanup duty for breaking school rules. Just then, Makhai accidentally bumped into Hestia with his tray.

He mumbled an apology. "Sorry . . . um . . . Helena."

Huh? Hestia had seen Makhai in here a thousand times, yet he didn't even know her name? "S'okay," she said quickly. She felt too shy to tell him her actual name, though.

"Here you go." Ms. Xena handed Makhai's friend Kydoimos a plate of food. The beefy-looking godboy regarded the plate and then the anteater-snouted lunch lady with an expression of suspicion. "You didn't drop any ants in this, did you?"

"Ha-ha. Good one," chortled Makhai as Ms. Xena dropped a plate of food onto his tray too.

Hestia cringed at the boys' rudeness, but Ms. Xena didn't miss a beat. Looking Kydoimos squarely in the eye, she retorted, "Why would I waste a delicacy like that on you?" Then she laughed in a series of snout-snorts.

Kydoimos sputtered a bit but seemed unable to

come up with a cool enough retort. "Right," he muttered at last. Then he and Makhai moved off with
their trays toward the tables. Hestia grinned. Two
points for Ms. Xena!

The lunch lady caught the grin and winked at her.
"Never let 'em get the best of you," she whispered.
Then she handed Hestia a plate with an extra large
helping of the yambrosia stew, some salad, and two
thick slices of the rosemary-olive bread.

"Thanks," said Hestia.

"See you later," said Ms. Xena.

Hestia smiled back, but her smile faded as she
turned toward the dining area. Time to find a seat.

It wasn't as if she didn't have any friends her
own age, she thought as she carried her tray past
tables. She did. A couple, anyway. Well, one, really.
Her roommate, Aglaia. She was the goddessgirl of

good health, or rather, the glow one gets from good health. Her smooth, pink cheeks seemed a testament to that. Only, Hestia hadn't seen much of Aglaia or her cheeks lately, except for during fifth period, when they had Hero-ology class together.

Ever since Aglaia had made friends with Hephaestus (the godboy of blacksmithing and metalworking), those two were always hanging out together. They both got a kick out of making various projects in the school's metalwork shop.

Hmm. Finding common interests with someone might be a good way for her to make friends, too. Did any kids at MOA like to cook? Hestia wondered. How was she supposed to find out? Interview them? As if!

She was passing the table now where some of the most popular godboys hung out. When Apollo, the godboy of prophecy (among other things), picked up a piece of her rosemary-olive bread, she slowed to watch him take a big bite.

"Wow!" He turned to his friend Dionysus. "This bread is mega-licious!"

"What? And you couldn't have predicted that before you took a bite?" teased Dionysus.

She smiled, and as she continued on, she imagined herself pausing to say, *Why, thanks!* [Cute giggle.] *I made the bread. So glad you like it.* Ha! Even if she could work up the nerve to say that, she wouldn't. Because she really did not like tooting her own horn.

Hestia was halfway across the cafeteria now. Her eyes darted here and there, looking for a place to sit, hoping to spot Aglaia. No such luck.

Usually, when Aglaia wasn't around, Hestia chose a table where she wouldn't be noticed. Like the one in the far corner of the cafeteria behind the column.

Or at a table with students who were doing home-work or reading assignments for their next class as they ate. She saw a couple of students doing that at one table ahead. If she sat in the empty chair across from them and pretended to do the same while she ate, it would be boring. But not as embarrassing as sitting somewhere eating by herself.

No! She took a deep breath, her eyes scanning other tables. Today she was going to make good on the first item on her new list. She would sit with someone she didn't know—or didn't know very well, anyway. And talk to them. Maybe say, like, twenty words. Or ten at least.

Still clutching her tray with both hands, she shut her eyes and kept slowly walking forward. When she bumped into a table, she would ask to sit there, she promised herself.

Before she could make good on that promise, however, her foot came down hard on something in her path.

"Ow!" shouted a boy's voice.

Her brown eyes flew open. In front of her stood the lizard godboy with the green-striped black hair from Crafts-ology. *Asca*. He was gritting his teeth as he balanced his full tray on the palm of one hand. In his other hand he held the tip of his long green tail. Oh no! She must've stepped on it!

Kydoimos had apparently seen it happen, because he was cracking up nearby.

"It's not funny," she murmured, totally embarrassed and apologetic for what she'd done. But she said it so quietly that no one heard, least of all Kydoimos.

Though she couldn't rightfully call Asca a friend, he'd at least smiled at her in Crafts-ology. He'd also said a few words to her in class from time to time. And now she'd stomped on his tail.

"I'm so sorry," she told him. "I wasn't looking where I was going. You all right?"

Asca flashed her a brief but pained smile. Then he nodded and let go of his tail, taking a more secure grip on his tray. "I'll live," he said as his tail unfurled behind him.

"But . . ."

"No biggie. Honest." He paused and cocked his head at her. "Hey, I know you. Hestia, right? I liked your kettle symbol thingie this morning."

Thrilled that he actually knew her name and relieved that his tail did seem okay, Hestia made a small joke at her own expense. "That makes one person." Then she added, "As a symbol, I guess a cooking pot lacks the pizzazz of, say, Zeus's thunderbolt. Though, come to think of it, a heavy iron kettle would make almost as good a weapon."

He laughed! "True. If you had good aim, you could fell an enemy with one. And then wear it as a helmet, too."

Hestia thought about saying, *Better yet, if you used it to cook something and then fed your enemies, you might be able to prevent a battle in the first place.* But for some reason the words froze in her mouth. She'd just remembered she was talking to a boy!

For a second or two, they stood awkwardly as if rooted to the cafeteria floor. Then a couple of boys called Asca over. "Well, later, kettle-girl," he said, grinning at her before moving off to eat with his friends.

Hestia sighed. Why hadn't she kept talking? She could have thanked him for liking her symbol. Or apologized one more time for stomping on her tail. Or said out loud what she'd been thinking about feeding enemies. But, as usual, she'd given way to her natural shyness and clammed up. *Double argh!*

She glanced around the cafeteria again. The tables seemed completely full now. The only empty chairs were at a small table just big enough for two at the back of the room. She headed for it. As she passed the table where the super popular friends Aphrodite, Athena, Persephone, and Artemis always sat, she heard someone say her name.

She turned her head to see if one of the girls was calling to her, but none of them was even looking at her. (No surprise. Why would they?) Thinking she'd only imagined her name being spoken, she took another step toward the small table at the back. Then she heard Artemis say, "Hestia? Oh, you mean that shy girl who hides in those hoods? Is that her name?"

Hestia felt as though Artemis, a superb archer, had just shot her through the heart with one of her famed silver arrows. An arrow she'd laced with a magical potion to hurt Hestia's feelings.

She did not *hide* in her hoods, Hestia thought as she hurried past the four goddessgirls. She wanted to get out of there before they realized she'd overheard and felt sorry for her or anything.

Then she recalled that she had indeed pulled her hood down to hide her face in Crafts-ology just that morning. Well, she thought, maybe she did occasionally sort of hide that way. And then she remembered doing it again in the lunch line just now. Okay, so maybe more than occasionally.

Still, she and Artemis had been in several classes together over the years. Hestia certainly knew Artemis's name! She knew more than that, she thought as she finally reached the empty table and sat.

She knew that Artemis had a crush on a mortal boy named Actaeon. And that her twin brother was Apollo, also an amazing archer. She knew all kinds of stuff about the four popular goddessgirls at MOA. And about lots of other students too. After all, Hestia had been at the Academy for four years now. Yet Makhai and Artemis still didn't know her name?

Thunk! Someone plopped a tray down across from her. It was Pheme, the goddessgirl of gossip. Hestia stared at her in surprise.

"Phew," said Pheme, running a hand through her short, spiky orange hair. "It's super crowded in here today!" As usual, her words formed cloud-letters that floated above her head for all to read. "You don't mind if I sit here, do you?"

Hestia couldn't help gaping at her. The gossipy girl had been in some classes with her over the years but had never spoken to her before. Maybe because there was nothing gossip-worthy about her. Nothing to put in the column Pheme wrote for *Teen Scrollazine*.

Remembering her vow to sit with someone new, Hestia finally managed to blurt out, "Of course I don't mind."

She smiled at Pheme. So what if the gossipy girl had only chosen to eat lunch with her because all the other tables were full? And so what if Pheme had asked to sit with her instead of the other way around? She'd fudge a little (as Ms. Okto would say). She'd count this encounter as fulfilling the first goal on her "change" list!

"Thanks," said Pheme, taking a seat. Then she cocked her head at Hestia. "I don't think I know you. Are you new to MOA, or just visiting?"

Argh! Really?

4

A Change of Plans

AT PHEME'S WORDS HESTIA'S SMILE FROZE AND her heart plummeted. It seemed that all her years of trying to remain invisible in classes had succeeded only too well. Counting Pheme that made three kids around here who didn't know who she was. At least Asca did, though.

"Actually," she told Pheme, making her voice super bright to hide her hurt, "I've been here since third grade. We had Science-ology together last year and Beauty-ology in fourth grade. My name's Hestia. *H-E-S-T-I-A*," she added helpfully.

Pheme's brown eyes blinked in surprise. Then her gaze shifted to Hestia's hood. "Oh yeah. Now I remember," she said at last. "You were that shy girl who sat in the back of the room in both classes and hardly said a word."

"Um . . . yeah . . . that was me," Hestia mumbled, squirming a little. What Pheme had said about her was sooo embarrassing! And every single word of it was now floating in cloud-letters above Pheme's head, where anyone in the cafeteria could see them. Hestia wished she had the nerve to raise her hands and brush those words away.

Seeming unaware of Hestia's distress, Pheme picked up the slice of rosemary-olive bread from her plate and bit into it. "Mmm, this is really good!"

"Thanks. I made it," Hestia announced. Her eyes widened in surprise. She hadn't intended to brag. The words had just popped out of her mouth with a will of their own. Maybe because she was feeling an uncharacteristic need for attention. For someone to notice her right now—just a little.

"Really?" said Pheme. Her eyes brightened with interest, and the tip of her tongue darted out to lick a crumb of bread from her orange-glossed lips.

"Mm-hm. It's a new recipe," Hestia went on proudly. "I made it just this morning."

Pheme leaned closer, folding her arms on the table. "So you work in the kitchen? Like, for punishment?"

Since Hestia had just taken her first bite of the bread, she simply nodded but then shook her head. Apollo had said her bread was good. And he was right. A bit too chewy, though. If she made it again, she'd let it rise longer so the texture was softer.

"Not for punishment. I love to cook," she explained after swallowing. "Ms. Hydra gave me permission to apprentice with the cafeteria ladies during third period. And sometimes I just go hang out there to try new recipes and stuff, too."

"Yeah?" Pheme said. Her warm tone invited Hestia to continue.

After a brief hesitation Hestia thought of something else to add. "I'm goddessgirl of the hearth. Guess that's why I've always been drawn to kitchens and cooking."

Except to Aglaia, she'd never revealed this much about herself before. But Pheme's interest made it easy to talk.

"Fascinating," Pheme said with enthusiasm. Between

bites of yambrosia she asked, "And have you created any other recipes? Besides the bread, I mean?"

"Sure. The yambrosia you're eating, for one thing," Hestia told her. Answering Pheme's questions was proving way less difficult than coming up with things to say on her own. "Celestial salad and nec-taroni are my creations too."

"I never knew that!" Pheme said in surprise. She grinned at Hestia. "And if there's something I don't know, it's a good bet others don't know it either." Her eyes were sparkling. "I bet readers of my *Teen Scrollazine* column would enjoy a story about you. Want to do an interview sometime?"

Startled by this unexpected question, Hestia pulled back from the edge of the table slightly. Pheme's interest was flattering, but would *'zine* read-ers really care to learn more about her? She wasn't a flashy goddess like Aphrodite, nor athletic like Artemis, nor brainy like Athena.

"I'm not sure if—" she started to answer.

"Please say yes," interrupted Pheme. "You're practically anonymous. An article about you in *Teen Scrollazine* will get you noticed. Plus, I really need a topic for this week's column."

In the past Hestia would have said no. Because in the past she wouldn't have wanted anyone's notice. But being anonymous was awfully close to being invisible, and hadn't she resolved to change? Making up her mind, she smiled at Pheme. "Okay. I'm up for it."

"Great!" Pheme exclaimed, waving her fork for emphasis like a cheerleader with a pom-pom. "How about after school?"

"You mean today?" Hestia squeaked.

"Got other plans?"

"Uh. No," Hestia replied, realizing how pathetic that must sound. Other students probably had their Friday afternoon all mapped out with fun trips to the Immortal Marketplace or to the Supernatural Market or playing out in the sports fields with friends. She, on the other hand, had been planning to rearrange the spices in the cafeteria kitchen in alphabetical order. "So where do you want to meet? At the library maybe? Or in my—"

"Oh, wait. I forgot!" Pheme interrupted again, snapping her fingers. "I'm flying north after school today to write a special feature about an ice sculpture contest."

Hestia's face fell. To her surprise she'd already begun looking forward to her interview. "That's okay," she said brightly, in an attempt to cover her disappointment. "An ice sculpture contest sounds—"

74

"Here's an idea," Pheme said, interrupting for the third time. "Why don't you come with me to the ice contest? We can do the interview on the way!"

"Really? Yeah, sure. I'd love to go," said Hestia. It would never have occurred to her to ask Pheme if she could go along, and she was overjoyed at the sudden invitation. Maybe in addition to the interview, spending time with Pheme would result in a new friendship!

"Is that hoodie you're wearing warm? The north can get kind of cold, with all that ice and stuff," Pheme told her as she spooned up the last of her yambrosia. "Also, just FYI, it will take about an hour to get to where we're going."

"Yeah, that's fine. I don't really get cold," Hestia replied, sipping her carton of nectar. This had something to do with her being able to make flames and being the goddess of the hearth, she'd always figured.

"Meet me in the courtyard an hour after school's out, okay?" Pheme said distractedly. Her attention had strayed in the direction of the tray return. Hestia glanced that way too, and saw that Pheme was watching Aphrodite. The fashionable goddessgirl had just emptied her tray and was heading out the cafeteria door, her sparkly pink handbag swinging from her shoulder.

"Okay," Hestia replied.

"Ta-ta for now, then," Pheme said, leaping up from the table. "I need to ask Aphrodite where she got that fabulous new handbag of hers. My readers will want to know!" Her small, iridescent orange wings flapped gently at her back, scooting her swiftly across the room.

"Bye!" Hestia called after her as the lyrebell chimed

the end of the lunch period. Since Pheme had forgotten to take her tray, Hestia stacked it on top of her own and then started across the room to empty them both. She was already mentally planning the snacks she'd bring along for their trip evening.

Halfway to the tray return, Asca appeared next to her. Only this time, he was semitransparent, which startled Hestia so much that she nearly dropped the trays. "Oh!" she said, rebalancing her hold on them.

"Sorry. Forgot I was blending in," he said. He began solidifying till he looked more like a boy than the cafeteria wall and was therefore easier to see. "'Camouflage' is the technical term," he said, grinning. He took Pheme's tray off the top of Hestia's stack to help her out.

How sweet! she thought. "Thanks," she told him.

He fell into step with her the rest of the way to the

tray return. "So Pheme's going to interview you for that scrollazine she writes for?" he asked. Seeing the question on her face, he pointed up, explaining, "I saw her cloud-words. Pretty much everybody could."

Hestia nodded as they dumped their trash and placed their trays in the return. "Oh, yeah. I sort of forgot about those when we were talking. Nice of her to want to interview me, though, huh?"

Before Asca could reply, Heracles called out to him from a group of guys about to leave the cafeteria. "Capture the flag game after school. On the farthest sports field. You in?"

Asca nodded in Heracles' direction. "Yeah. Later!"

With his skill at camouflage he was probably really good at games requiring stealth, thought Hestia. He could sneak up and steal the other team's flag, and they'd never even see him do it.

Asca's attention swung back to her again. "About that interview. Pheme doesn't always get her facts straight, and well, just be careful what you say to her." With a quick smile and a wave, he left the cafeteria, changing color till he blended in with the walls again.

Hestia watched him go—or stared at the place where she thought he might be, anyway. It was hard to tell since he was now camouflaged. *I don't know what you mean,* she wanted to call after him. Why the warning? Had he been speaking from experience?

Vaguely, she remembered reading an interview Pheme had done with Asca in one of her columns a while back. Maybe once she was in her room again she could find the issue among the stack of 'zines on the shelf above her desk and reread it for details. Hoping she hadn't made a mistake in agreeing to the interview, she hurried off to her next class.

5

Preparations

As soon as school was out, Hestia rushed to the cafeteria. Ms. Xena was sitting at a table in the now empty dining area near the snacks counter. She was reading a scrollazine called *Exotic Eats*. Hestia wondered if it had recipes for things like cricket crêpes or flea flan. Hestia preferred bugless fare herself, thank you very much. Ms. Xena was who she was, however. Whatever she liked to eat was her own beeswax.

Ms. Xena looked up as Hestia reached into a bowl for a couple of apples. "Snacks for a trip," Hestia explained. "Pheme invited me to go to an ice sculpture contest with her."

"Nice!" Ms. Xena approved. "I didn't know the two of you had become friends." Letting her scrollazine snap shut, she got up from the table. "You should take some of those chocolate ambrosia bars you made a few days ago too."

"I thought they were all gone," Hestia said.

"I saved a few," Ms. Xena told her.

Hestia followed her to the kitchen. "Pheme's not really a friend. Not yet, anyway. She only asked me along because she wants to interview me for *Teen Scrollazine*."

"Really? An interview?" Ms. Xena said as the two of them pushed through the swinging door and into the kitchen. "That's pretty terrific." She went straight to a cupboard where she'd apparently hidden away a few of the chocolate ambrosia bars.

"Hope so," Hestia said, watching her rummage around on a shelf inside the cupboard. "Asca—he's that godboy with the lizard tail—told me I should be careful with what I say to her. Because she doesn't always get her facts straight."

"That's likely making a mountain out of an anthill," said Ms. Xena, at last handing her a papyrus-wrapped package of two ambrosia bars. "All publicity is good publicity. I read that somewhere."

"Probably in Pheme's *Teen Scrollazine* column," Hestia joked.

Ms. Xena chuckled. "You could be right." She cocked her head at Hestia. "It may not have occurred to you, but an interview in Pheme's column could be just the publicity you need to help you win that Service to Humankind Award."

"Think so?" said Hestia. It honestly *hadn't* occurred to her. It was a nice thought, but her only real service to humankind was her creation of public hearths back when she was eight. Those hearths ensured that there would always be a central place in every town for villagers to get fire for cooking and heating. Useful, to be sure. But, like kettles, hearths would make a terrible symbol. They would be hard to draw, lacked pizzazz, and didn't really stack up against other students' contributions. Or so it seemed to her.

Ms. Xena nodded. "Couldn't hurt," she said before heading back out to the cafeteria to return to her reading.

Spotting a few leftover slices of rosemary-olive bread on the counter, Hestia began making sandwiches to take along, since she and Pheme would likely miss dinner.

When she finally left the kitchen with her bag of food in hand, there was still about a half hour left till she needed to meet Pheme. She decided to go upstairs to let her roomie know where she'd be. However, Aglaia wasn't around as she entered their small room.

It had identical beds, desks, and closets on either side. A window directly across from the door over-looked the front of the Academy and the marble courtyard down below. A quick peek showed her that Pheme wasn't out there early.

After dropping the bag of food onto her bed, Hestia decided to scribble a note to her roommate. Aglaia might worry where she was, since Hestia rarely went anywhere. But before she did that, she pulled out the recipe card with the list of tasks she'd assigned herself that morning and quickly reread them.

A smile came over her face as she realized she'd accomplished three of the five tasks already! She'd sat with Pheme—well, technically, Pheme had sat with her. But still, she'd made an effort to befriend the gossipy girl, so same diff. And she'd chatted with Asca, a boy. And she'd said yes to Pheme's interview request and invitation to the ice sculpture contest.

Grabbing a feather pen from her desk, Hestia checked off the completed tasks with a flourish.

1. SIT WITH SOMEONE NEW AT LUNCH. ✓

2. STAND UP FOR SOMEONE.

3. TALK TO A BOY. ✓

4. TRY SOMETHING I'D NORMALLY SAY NO TO. ✓

5. TAKE A TRULY BIG, BOLD COOKING RISK!

Just two more to go! She slipped the list back into the pocket of her chiton. Spotting the stack of old *Teen Scrollazine*s on her shelf, she remembered she wanted to search for the column that had something about Asca in it.

As she pored over several scrollazines, trying to find the right one, she came across a reader poll Pheme had conducted a while back. In the poll, mortals on Earth had chosen a Best of MOA list, naming their top twenty Mount Olympus Academy students and their best traits. Among the ten girls named, Athena had been voted Most Academic; Aphrodite, Most Glamorous; Artemis, Best Athlete; and Pandora, Most School Spirit.

Naturally, Hestia had received no mention at all. If there had been a Most Invisible category, she could have won that one hands down, though, she thought. And that was no joke!

Two issues later, she found the column she'd been looking for in a scrollazine that had come out only a month and a half ago. In her interview with Asca, Pheme had discussed his skill at camouflage. Her article ended with a warning to readers:

If you should see Ascalabus, be careful not to startle him. If frightened, his lizard tail could break off, and then he would be left with just a stump!

Whoa! Was that true? wondered Hestia. She plunked onto her bed, her mouth open. Lucky thing she hadn't startled him so much that his tail had broken off. But wait. Asca had said that Pheme didn't always get her facts straight. So was the tail thing true? Or not?

Snap! She let the scrollazine roll itself up and then put it back on the shelf with the others. She wished she could ask Asca for the truth about his tail, but she wouldn't want to hurt his feelings by bringing up a sore subject. Sore in more than one way, since a broken tail would really hurt.

Well, she'd just be careful what she said to Pheme, but not worry too much about it. Like Ms. Xena had said, "All publicity is good publicity." So not doing the interview would be the worst possible choice if she wanted to shed some of her invisibility.

Glancing out the window, Hestia saw from the sundial below that she needed to meet Pheme in a few minutes. She grabbed a piece of papyrus and a feather pen to scribble a note, but then her roommate appeared in the doorway.

"Oh, there you are," Hestia said. "I was just going to write you a note. Pheme invited me to go to an ice sculpture contest with her. I didn't want you to wonder where I was."

Aglaia's pretty brown eyes lit up, and she smiled.

"Awesome!" she enthused. "Pheme's fun, so that should be, well, fun!" She giggled.

"Uh, thanks," said Hestia. She could tell that Aglaia was genuinely happy for her, but couldn't she have acted a little sorry that they wouldn't be able to hang out together this evening? Maybe her room-mate thought it was about time Hestia made other friends to do stuff with. Had she been depending too much on Aglaia?

"By the way," Aglaia added as she kicked off her sandals. "I'm sleeping over with Calliope in her room tonight."

"Oh. Well, have fun," said Hestia. Calliope was a younger sister of MOA's Science-ology teacher, Muse Urania. Like Amphitrite, Calliope had only just started at the Academy, but it sounded like she was already making new friends. Hestia felt a tiny stab of jealousy. What if Aglaia's new friendship with Calliope meant that she would have even less time for Hestia from now on?

Remembering it was time to go, Hestia said a quick bye, picked up the bag of food from her bed, and quickly made her way downstairs. In the Academy's entryway she shucked off her everyday sandals and grabbed a pair of winged ones from the basket by the big front doors. She slipped the sandals on. The silver wings at their heels were bound together, but she wouldn't need to free them till she was ready to fly. After pushing through the doors, she took the granite steps downward.

There were lots of students outside enjoying the sunny afternoon. Some were sitting with friends on the steps. Others were reading, studying, or visiting on benches around the marble-tiled courtyard below.

Still more students were standing around, laughing or talking in small groups.

It was good flying weather. The air was so still that the anemometer in the middle of the courtyard—a gadget that measured wind speed—was barely moving. The figures of four wind-brothers—the godboys Boreas, Zephyr, Notus, and Eurus—had been carved onto the gadget's main post by a famous sculptor named Pygmalion. Their cheeks were round and puffed, as if blowing out swirls of wind.

Hestia was halfway down the steps when she saw Pheme. The goddessgirl of gossip was easy to spot, with her bright orange hair and dazzling orange wings. She was fluttering from group to group, sharing the newest gossip. She was the least shy goddess Hestia knew, absolutely unafraid to approach anyone and start a conversation.

I can learn a thing or two from her, Hestia thought. And with that in mind, she zipped down the rest of the steps and all the way across the courtyard to Pheme's side.

Since the girl's back was to her, Hestia tapped her on the shoulder. "I'm here," she announced breathlessly. "Ready to go?"

6
The Journey North

Y EAH, I'M READY!" SAID PHEME, TURNING TOWARD

Hestia. She nodded to the group she was with,

which included Aphrodite, Persephone, Apollo,

and Artemis. All of them stared curiously at Hestia,

making her flush. If any of these very familiar immor-

tals asked who she was, she was going to scream. Not

really, but she'd sort of want to.

"In case you don't know her, this is Hestia," Pheme

told the others before anyone could say anything. Grinning, she spelled the name out, just as Hestia had done at lunch, "*H-E-S-T-I-A*." Of course, cloud-letters were already rising above Pheme's head, making the spelling completely unnecessary. "The only free seat in the cafeteria at lunch today was across from her," Pheme went on. "So that's how we finally met up!"

The only free seat in the cafeteria? Ducking back into her hood a little, Hestia flushed even more. Her light freckles were probably turning beet red! She looked up as cloud-letters spread Pheme's every word far and wide. The gossipy girl surely didn't mean it the way it sounded, but her introduction had made Hestia sound like a loser. Spelled *L-O-S-E-R*.

There was an awkward pause. Then Persephone smiled at Hestia. "So where are you guys off to?" she asked politely.

Before Hestia could even open her mouth, Pheme blurted out, "To an ice sculpture contest up north. I'm going to write a special article about it for *Teen Scrollazine*." She smiled at Hestia. "Come on, girl, let's get going!" She said good-bye for both of them, and they started across the courtyard.

If she became friends with Pheme, she'd probably never have to speak at all, Hestia thought wryly. Pheme would do all the talking. It would make things easy, but that wasn't really what she was hoping for in a new friendship.

Bending, Hestia loosened the laces that kept the silver wings at the heels of her sandals still. The sandals' straps magically twined themselves around her ankles, and the freed wings began to flap. Pheme had no need for winged sandals since she had real wings. Putting on a burst of speed, the two girls took off.

Flying high, they whooshed over the top of the Academy. The magnificent building stood five stories high. Its polished stone walls and tall Ionic columns sparkled in the sunlight. But what Hestia loved best were the shallow sculptures celebrating various historical feats of the immortals that were carved just below the Academy's peaked rooftop.

In her opinion there was no grander place in the world than MOA.

After passing over the Academy, the two goddessgirls flew over many small farms, villages, and towns, but there were fewer of these the farther north they went. It was all quite exciting to Hestia, since she rarely traveled. Unlike most immortals, who were always dashing off to do amazing things, she supposed she was a homebody at heart. Still, she was in an adventurous mood today and ready to see something new!

Pheme didn't ask her any interview questions right away. Instead, they chatted about classes, other students, and the sights they saw below.

Time passed quickly, and soon a gray-black sea churned below them. Pheme shivered and pulled her cloak close around her. There were small holes in the back of it for her wings, Hestia noticed.

Pheme pointed downward. "Brr. Look at those jagged white-and-blue icebergs floating in that water. I hope we don't turn into ice sculptures ourselves before we get to where we're going."

Hestia laughed, but as usual she didn't find the cold bothersome. She raised the arm she'd looped her bag's handles over. "Will snacks help? I brought some."

Pheme nodded enthusiastically. "Good thinking. I'm starving."

Honk! Honk! As Hestia reached into her bag, a

flock of snow geese appeared in the sky and came straight toward them. "Incoming!" she yelled.

Pheme's eyes whipped to look ahead, her expression alarmed. With expert moves both girls leaned this way and that, dodging around the flock to avoid a crash.

"Phew! That was close. I think we really deserve these snacks now, don't you?" said Hestia once they were safely past the birds. She pulled out one of the sandwiches she'd made and handed it to Pheme. Then she pulled the other one out for herself.

"Definitely," said Pheme. Her wings flapped rapidly to keep her aloft as she took a bite. "Mmm. This tastes awesome! What's inside?"

Hestia glowed with pride. "It's a spread I made up with various nuts, soft cheese, herbs, and a few other ingredients." She took a bite of her sandwich too. "Ooh! It is yummy!" They both laughed. Then she cocked her head. "Maybe I'll add a little bit of onion next time I make it, though."

As they munched, Pheme began prompting her with questions. Hestia was careful in her replies at first. But she quickly loosened up. Pheme was so easy to talk to. This friend thing wasn't turning out to be all that hard, she decided happily.

To Hestia's delight, Pheme ate every last bite of the sandwich, oohing and aahing over it. After they munched the apples she'd brought, Hestia passed Pheme a chocolate ambrosia bar.

At her very first bite of it, a look of dreamy pleasure came over Pheme's face. "Scrumptious!" she exclaimed. "Your recipe too?"

Hestia nodded. It really made her happy to see others enjoy the food she made. "I baked them two days ago and thought they'd all been eaten. Luckily, Ms. Xena had hidden two away in a kitchen cupboard and said we could have them."

Pheme arched an eyebrow. "Who's Ms. Xena?"

"You know, Ms. Xenarthra," Hestia said, thinking Pheme must not have known Ms. Xena's shortened name. When Pheme still appeared confused, Hestia added, "She's one of the cafeteria ladies. The one with the snout."

"Oh. Her. The anteater lady who goes around sucking up crumbs?" Pheme made an ick face.

"Mm-hm," said Hestia. "She does have odd eating habits, but she's totally cool. She helped me get my kitchen apprenticeship."

"Really?" said Pheme. Her eyes lit up with interest. "Tell me more."

It felt good that someone was curious to know

more about the things Hestia cared about, and Ms. Xena was definitely one of those things. So as the two girls flew on, Hestia told Pheme all about the cafeteria lady. She included some funny stories about cooking mishaps, like the over-peppered yambrosia that she, Ms. Okto, and Ms. Xena had all laughed over. She smiled with pleasure when Pheme laughed too.

"Okay it I mention Ms. Okto and Ms. Xena in the article I'm going to write about you?" Pheme asked. "I think readers would love to hear about those ladies."

Hestia hesitated. Pheme had been questioning her so skillfully that she'd sort of forgotten that this was about gathering information for an article. She'd just thought they were talking. For a fraction of a second she remembered what Asca had said about Pheme. Even though she wasn't really cold,

Hestia clasped the neck of her hood to tighten it over her head as the wind grew brisker.

Thing was, she kind of wanted Pheme's approval. Besides, she was pretty sure Ms. Xena would enjoy seeing herself in *Teen Scrollazine*. And that lady deserved some recognition. She worked so hard, yet Pheme and probably others didn't know her name anymore than they knew Hestia's. Unless there was a problem in the cafeteria and a student needed to complain to someone about it, the kitchen staff was likely as invisible as Hestia was! It would be good for students to find out how awesome Ms. Okto and Ms. Xena were.

"I think that might be cool," Hestia said at last. "They read your column in *Teen Scrollazine*. Or at least Ms. Xena does. But maybe I should ask them first if it's—"

"Hey, I think we're here!" Pheme announced, her words drowning Hestia's out.

102

Hestia glanced down. Below them, a flat sheet of ice stretched out as big as an island. It was dotted with oversized, frozen statues of gods and goddesses. Lots of people were milling around the statues, studying them.

"Look! It's *Zeus*! A statue of him, I mean," said Pheme, pointing. Sure enough, among the towering, glittering ice sculptures, there was one of the MOA principal. He sat atop his winged horse, Pegasus, with his arm raised to hurl a mighty thunderbolt.

"Wow, it's amazing! And there's one of Athena," said Hestia, forgetting all about their previous conversation. "It's so lifelike. Let's go in closer."

The girls landed just in time to hear someone with a megaphone announce, "Judges! You may begin!"

Hestia's jaw dropped when three figures suddenly burst out of an igloo to zoom across the ice toward the sculptures. They looked like hairy haystack triplets on ice skates. The peppy gray haystacks varied in height—one short, one medium-size, and one tall. Carrying clipboards in their hay-hands, they glided toward the sculptures. Never coming to a full stop, they visited each one in turn, whizzing around it and making notes before moving on.

This was odd enough. But the weirdest thing about the figures was that they had only one eyeball between them, and they kept passing it around. It seemed to be the only way they could see!

"Those are the judges?" Hestia asked in astonishment as she tried to find her footing on the ice. She attempted to grab on to an icy pedestal to get her balance, but her hands just slid right off.

Pheme nodded, sliding around too. Her head was turning this way and that, probably scouting for news scoops. "Yep. They're the Gray Ladies," she said. "Also known as the MOA counselors."

"Oh yeah. I've heard of them," Hestia said. "Look at them go! They're like champion skaters or something. I'm having trouble just standing and walking on this slippery ice without falling."

But she'd spoken too soon. Just then the shortest of the Gray Ladies went hurtling toward the backside of a statue. Gasps sounded as onlookers feared an imminent crash. At the last minute the short lady crouched low, though, and slid through the legs of the statue to get to its other side.

"Smooth save!" someone cheered, and the Ladies all grinned and waved. It was then that Hestia noticed that one of them had a single big white tooth. The others had no teeth at all!

"Besides knowing a lot about ice, those Ladies are pretty opinionated," Pheme told her. "That's probably why they were asked to judge this contest. Their office is an igloo only a few mi—" She stopped midword, her interest abruptly caught by something, or someone, across the ice.

"Pygmalion!" she shouted excitedly. "I wonder if he sculpted any of these statues. I've got to ask him what he thinks of them. My readers will be dying to know!"

As Pheme skate-walked over to the famous sculptor, she called back over her shoulder to Hestia, "Catch up with you later, okay?"

"Okay." Hestia really wanted to see the statues, and it would be nice to do so in quiet. Pheme was anything but that! Hestia wandered up one row and down the next, pausing before each of the sculptures to admire the artistry of the sculptors who had made them. She slipped and slid a lot at first, but after a while she got used to walking on ice. You just had to take careful steps and not hurry.

Unless you were a haystack on ice skates, that was. She watched the school counselors jump one after the other over a life-size chariot carved from ice and then twirl around a sculpture of a three-headed dog while making notes on their clipboards.

The detail in the sculptures was incredible. Hestia gasped in amazement when she came upon one of Heracles fighting the fierce Nemean lion, which had once terrorized a town. The figures were posed so that Heracles was brandishing his enormous club as the wild-eyed lion lunged for him. Every muscle in the mortal boy's raised arm was clearly defined. Wow!

There were monsters carved from ice too. Hestia recognized them from studies in Beast-ology class at MOA. The creature with a fire-breathing lion's head, a goat's body, and a serpent tail was a Chimera. And the one-headed, two-armed, three-bodied, four-winged, six-legged beast was a Geryon. Luckily, it wasn't real, because Geryons had very stinky breath. There were also scaly dragons of various shapes and sizes.

Along the very last row of sculptures, Hestia came upon the especially well-executed sculpture of Athena she and Pheme had glimpsed as they'd flown in. The icy Athena was dressed in battle gear and was frozen in the act of springing out of the top of Zeus's head—which was actually how she'd been born. Sounded weird, but events like that were pretty normal when it came to immortals. For instance, Aphrodite had been born from sea foam!

Lost in wonder at the beauty of the sculpture, Hestia was startled when the Gray Ladies glided up with their clipboards in hand to surround her.

Slipping on the ice, she fell backward. Ouch!

Her eyes went from one haystack lady to the next. They were circling her now on their skates, passing their big round detachable eye among them to study her as closely as they had the statues on display. Each time the eye was popped into a face, it made an icky squelching sound.

As Hestia scrambled to her feet again, the tall Gray Lady spoke up. She was in charge of the tooth now. Apparently, it was what allowed her to talk. "Name two art forms that take a long time to create and yet always disappear in a short time," she demanded.

"Huh? Is this some kind of quiz?" mumbled Hestia. Still zooming around her, they all three nodded. A quiz after school hours didn't seem fair, but maybe this was important to them, so she did her best to figure out an answer.

"Well, these ice sculptures are an art form, right? They must take a long time to carve," Hestia said, gesturing around her. "But they'll melt quickly when warmer weather comes."

A small gap opened up between two of the haystacks. Hestia took advantage of the opening and started to edge away. However, the medium-size haystack grabbed the tooth and then zoomed around the circle to block her exit, asking, "Does their short-lived nature remind you of another art form, Hestia?"

Hestia's eyes widened, and she took a step backward and then had to spin her arms to keep from falling again. "How do you know my n-name?" Students she'd been in classes with at MOA for years still didn't know who she was, and she'd never even seen the Gray Ladies before today.

110

The small haystack grabbed the tooth and made a tsking sound. "We're the MOA counselors. We know a lot of things about students attending the Academy. It's part of our job."

Hestia eyed them warily. What else did they know about her? she wondered. That she didn't have many friends? That she liked cooking? Then suddenly she had the rest of the answer to their pop quiz.

"Cooking!" she exclaimed. "Preparing food takes a long time. Yet it gets gobbled down fast. And like ice melts, food melts in people's mouths." Ice sculptures and cooking. Both were art forms, but fleeting ones.

"Bingo!" The medium-size haystack, who had grabbed the tooth again, grinned at her.

Although the one-toothed grin was a bit weird, even somewhat scary, Hestia found herself grinning back.

7

Armor

THE TALL GRAY LADY TOOK POSSESSION OF THE eye and the tooth now. *Squish!* As the other two whizzed around them, she looked Hestia up and down and then gestured toward the Athena sculpture. "Do you like it, goddessgirl of the hearth?" she asked.

Hestia blinked. These counselors knew her goddessgirl title, too? "Um, it's cool," she told them when she finally found her tongue. "All the sculptures are. But I think this one might be my favorite."

The tall Gray Lady cocked her head. "Why is that?" she asked, before passing the eye and tooth to the shortest sister, who was reaching for them as she zoomed by.

Hestia thought a minute. Then she said, "The detail in Athena's armor is amazing, but it's the aliveness of the figures that I like most. The expression on Zeus's face is so . . . well . . . complicated. It seems to show equal parts love, pride, and pain."

The short Gray Lady nodded in approval. "Explain further, please."

Hestia considered. "Well, everyone knows Zeus loves Athena. I mean, he's her dad. And he calls her this cute nickname sometimes—Theeny. He's obviously proud of her, too. She's so smart. I think her braininess and wisdom are symbolized in this statue by her springing from Zeus's head. Still, I'm guessing that it was a real pain for Zeus when that happened. A massive headache, right? Plus . . ." She paused for a moment.

"Go on," said the medium-size Gray Lady, who now had the tooth back. The other two haystacks paused and leaned in to better hear. At least they didn't have to share an ear, Hestia thought. Why did they care about her opinion, anyway? She looked around for a possible escape. No chance. Where was Pheme?

"O-okay." What choice did she have? They weren't going to let her go until they were satisfied she'd dug deep to answer their questions. "It's just that . . . well . . . there's another side to the pain. Because even though Zeus is the most powerful god of all, he can't protect Athena from every prob-

lem she'll face. You know, stuff like school dr.
making mistakes, giant fire-breathing monsters s
might run into. And that's probably a real pain for
someone like Zeus, who is used to being able to control everything."

As the words spilled from her lips, Hestia's face
brightened with sudden insight. "So that must be
what's symbolized by Athena being born with her
own armor. It's to protect herself!"

"Interesting," said the short Gray Lady, who now
had the eye and the tooth again. "Your own armor
has served you well, but perhaps now is the time to
shed it?"

"Huh? What armor?" Hestia asked, bewildered.
She didn't even own a helmet!

But the short Gray Lady didn't explain. After pop-
ping the tooth from her mouth, she passed it to the

medium-size Lady. That one said something even more puzzling. "When you hide your light under a cooking pot, you deprive others of your gifts."

Light? Cooking pot? Gifts? What was all that supposed to mean? Hestia wondered as the shortest lady passed both the eye and the tooth to the tallest sister.

"And you also cheat yourself," the tallest remarked in a tone of conclusion.

"Uh, okay. Thanks. I'll remember that," Hestia said, totally confused.

To her relief the guy with the megaphone suddenly summoned the three haystacks. With quick nods to her, they finally whirled, twirled, and skated off toward a grandstand festooned with flags and ribbons.

"Bye! Awesome advice!" Hestia called after them. But really, in her opinion those Ladies were beyond goofy. Before she could consider their strange words any further, Pheme appeared beside her.

"Guess what?" the orange-haired girl said, her eyes sparkling with excitement. "Pygmalion agreed to give me an interview as soon as the winners are announced, which should be in just a few—"

"Your attention, please!" the contest announcer shouted through his megaphone, drowning her out. "Our illustrious judges have tallied their results!"

Swiveling her head, Hestia located the announcer standing beside the three Gray Ladies on a platform in front of the grandstand. A hush came over the crowd as he brought the megaphone up to his mouth once more. "It is time now to name the winners of this year's annual ice sculpture contest!"

Taking turns, the Gray Ladies borrowed the tooth and the microphone to announce the third-, then second-, then first-place winners. The three-headed dog sculpture, whose title was *Cerberus*, won third prize.

"Hades will be thrilled when he hears about this," Pheme leaned over to whisper. Hades, who was Persephone's crush, also attended MOA. He was godboy of the Underworld, and Cerberus was his pet dog. That fierce-looking creature guarded the entrance to the Underworld and kept shades—spirits of the dead, that is—from escaping.

Hestia cheered extra loudly when her favorite ice sculpture, *The Birth of Athena*, took second place and a female sculptor stepped up to claim the prize.

Heracles' First Labor, whose creator turned out to be none other than the world-renowned Pygmalion, won first. It was the sculpture Hestia had admired of Heracles battling the Nemean lion.

Later, as an artist from the *Greekly Weekly News* sketched a picture of Pygmalion's winning statue, Hestia listened in on Pheme's brief interview with the great sculptor.

"Were you surprised to win?" Pheme asked him.

"Not at all," Pygmalion told her with a haughty sniff. "This was only an amateur contest, so there was really no competition for someone of my stature in the art world. I only entered because the contest organizers begged me to."

A few minutes later, after the two girls began their trip back to MOA, Pheme imitated the manner of Pygmalion's speaking. "Those other sculptors are losers without a scrap of talent compared to me," she said with her chin up and her nose in the air.

Grinning, Hestia added, "They are not worthy even to lick my sandals."

Both girls burst out laughing, which caused them to bobble around in the air. In fact, Hestia laughed so hard, she actually did a frontward flip and had to right herself. Pygmalion was a brilliant sculptor, but he was also very arrogant.

"I kind of hoped *The Birth of Athena* would take first, but at least it won second," Hestia commented as they flew back over the gray-black sea.

"What's good about second place?" Pheme said with a snort. "All the publicity and acclaim go to the winner!"

"Huh? No way. The Athena sculptor almost won," Hestia argued. "Hundreds admired and enjoyed that woman's work. Her talent made them happy. It made me—probably others too—pause to think. That's the stuff that's important."

"Ha!" said Pheme, unconvinced. But then she

changed the subject. "So I saw you talking to the Gray Ladies. They're weird, right?"

Hestia nodded. "I'll say. Imagine having to share your only eyeball and tooth with your sisters! I wonder how they eat. It would be hard to chew food with only one tooth."

"Maybe they just take turns sipping milkshakes," said Pheme.

"Yeah, in a single glass where they share one straw," Hestia added.

The girls laughed again, bobbling about in the air as before. "Those ladies don't just look and act weird, they also said some really weird stuff to me," Hestia confided once she'd straightened. "Stuff that doesn't make any sense." After a pause she added, "Only I'm wondering if it was supposed to have been helpful advice since they're counselors."

"What kind of advice?" encouraged Pheme. In her excitement to hear what Hestia would reveal, her glittery orange wings beat double-time.

"They said I wear armor, for one thing," Hestia told her. A sudden gust of wind blew her hood back. She tugged it forward as she then went on to repeat not just the armor comment but the cooking-pot comment also, and the warning not to cheat herself. "I didn't ask for their advice. Especially unclear advice like that."

"Yeah, but like you said yourself, they're counselors," said Pheme. "Giving advice is what they do. And their suggestions usually make sense after you consider them awhile."

As the girls began to fly over land again, Hestia wondered if Pheme had ever received advice from the Gray Ladies. She didn't ask, however. She sensed it might be a touchy subject. When another gust of wind flipped back the hood of her chiton, Hestia pulled it into place again.

Pheme glanced at her. "If you don't get cold, why do you always wear hoods?"

Hestia shrugged. "I just like them. They make me feel more comfortable. Snuggly. And . . . safer, somehow."

Pheme's eyebrows shot up. "Safer? From what?"

"I don't know," said Hestia, looking away. "From stuff I don't want to deal with, I guess. Getting called on in class. Being noticed when I don't want to be. I'm kind of shy, and a hood is protection in a way."

"Like a helmet?" Pheme asked.

Hestia nodded. "Or a shield. Any type of—"

"Armor!" they both blurted at once.

"'Your own armor has served you well, but perhaps

now is the time to shed it?'" Hestia said, reciting the short Gray Lady's advice again, word for word. "So maybe they were trying to tell me I should get rid of the hoods on my chitons."

Pheme regarded Hestia thoughtfully as they flew closer and closer to Mount Olympus, which now towered on the horizon. "I don't get being shy. I mean, it's so easy to talk. For me, the bigger the audience, the better."

Hestia grinned at her. "Yeah! I've noticed! You're lucky. I wish I were that way."

"If everybody were like me, no one could get a word in edgewise, though," Pheme said matter-of-factly as they approached the Academy at the top of Mount Olympus. "Still, maybe you just need a little boost so people can start getting to know you." She licked her lips eagerly. "And I'm just the goddessgirl to help with that. Soon everyone at MOA will know not only your name but everything about you!"

She reached over and gave Hestia an excited hug just as they hit some bumpy air currents. They jumped apart, working to stay aloft.

Hestia's stomach gave a lurch. It had nothing to do with the bumpy air currents, however. She'd always been a very private person, so the idea of others knowing "everything" about her kind of freaked her out. But if she were to be honest, it was also a little thrilling. And it was, after all, what the Gray Ladies had seemed to advise. Even Ms. Xena approved of publicity. So Pheme would be doing Hestia a favor by giving her some. Right?

8

Pizzazz

Hestia spent most of Saturday in the cafeteria kitchen. Between helping out with lunch and dinner, she and Ms. Okto brainstormed ideas for a menu for next Saturday's banquet. Unfortunately— or fortunately, depending on how you looked at it— Chef Soterides came by to offer his opinions too.

"Zeus has already approved my main course," the chef informed them. "All that's left to decide are the appetizers and dessert. For appetizers I suggest we serve goat cheese crostini with roasted grapes; shrimp-and-tomato tarts; and a basil-ambrosia yogurt dip with baked pita wedges."

Ms. Okto folded all eight of her arms into four pairs and glared at him. "And just how are we supposed to find time to do all these fancy-pants appetizers in addition to the rest of the meal?"

The chef raised an eyebrow. "Not up to the challenge?"

Ignoring the obvious jab, Ms. Okto continued to glower at him. "A big platter of hambrosia roll-ups ought to do the trick. Takes a lot less time too."

Chef Soterides gave a sniff. "Uninspired and boring," he pronounced.

Ms. Okto pursed her lips. "Oh yeah? Well, I find your suggestions pompous and fussy!"

Caught in the cross fire, Hestia and Ms. Xena

stood near the two cooks, looking back and forth between them as they sparred.

Suddenly, the chef snapped his fingers. "We'll carve turnips into the shape of little anchovy fish. Boil them, dunk them in oil, and then decorate each to look just like the real thing, using salt and poppy seeds."

"I knew it! I knew you'd suggest those things. Stealing my ideas, just like back in cooking school."

Chef Soterides did a double take. "Oktopia? Is that you?" His face broke out into a huge smile. "I haven't seen you since we graduated. What's it been? Twenty years?"

"Twenty-three," Ms. Okto corrected him. Then, sounding miffed, she said, "I can't believe you didn't remember me till now. How many other eight-handed cooks have you come across all these years?"

"None," the chef admitted sheepishly. His eyes

darted to Hestia and Ms. Xena, who were listening in unabashedly. Quickly, they both got busy doing small kitchen tasks, so as not to appear too nosy.

"Seriously, Oktopia," Soterides said. "I've never known anyone as handy in a kitchen as you."

To Hestia's surprise Ms. Okto let out a giggle. "Stop trying to butter me up, Soty. I still haven't forgiven you for claiming that anchovy idea as your own, you know."

Hestia grinned at Ms. Xena, whispering, "Soty?" Ms. Xena shrugged and grinned back.

"I was desperate," the chef said now in a pleading tone. "You've got to understand. King Nikomedes was interviewing me for a job. The cost of failure was . . ." He drew a finger across his throat.

"Hmph!" said Ms. Okto. Then, appearing to take pity on him at last, she added, "Fine. The faux anchovies will do for an appetizer. Now, how about Hestia's chocolate ambrosia bars for dessert?"

Hestia had made another batch of them just before lunch, and now Ms. Okto handed one to the chef. Hestia watched anxiously as he took a bite. He chewed, then frowned.

Before he could say a word, Ms. Okto put seven hands on her hips. The eighth hand shook a wooden stirring spoon at him. "You'd better not insult Hestia's work. Everyone loves those bars!"

Soterides glanced between Ms. Okto and Hestia. "Absolutely scrumptious!" he declared. "But are they special enough?"

Hestia wrinkled her brow and spoke up before the cafeteria ladies could. "You're probably right," she said. "The dessert for such a mega-important banquet should have . . . pizzazz."

"Precisely!" agreed the chef. And for the next fifteen minutes he and Ms. Okto argued over dessert ideas.

In the end the lunch lady cocked her head. "How about if we leave the dessert to Hestia? It can be a surprise. To us and to everyone else."

"But this is unheard of!" Soterides exclaimed. "You can't be seri—"

"Ahem!" interrupted Ms. Okto. There were daggers in her eyes. "You. Owe. Me. One," she said, pronouncing each word loudly and distinctly.

The chef heaved a big sigh. "Yes, that's true," he conceded. "Very well."

"Really?" said Hestia, looking from one to the other. "Are you sure?" she asked Ms. Okto.

"Wouldn't have suggested it if I weren't," she said. "You've proved yourself an excellent cook many times over. I trust that whatever you come up with will be a huge hit."

"Sure it will," Ms. Xena chimed in.

Hestia beamed at them. "Thanks. I won't let any of you down."

"I should hope not," the chef couldn't seem to resist saying. "I can't imagine what Zeus might do if displeased. He's a zillion times more powerful than King Nikomedes, after all." Then, in case his meaning hadn't been clear enough, he drew a line across his throat with a finger.

"Pshaw," said Ms. Okto. "Don't let Soty worry you, Hestia. He's as nutty as a fruitcake if he thinks Zeus isn't going to love what you create."

Hestia nodded. She wasn't really worried about pleasing Zeus. As everyone knew, the principal had a major sweet tooth. No, it was Chef Soterides she was most worried about. Ms. Okto was counting on her to prove herself to him!

Back in her room after dinner that night, Hestia sat at her desk to brainstorm dessert ideas. However, everything she came up with—from cakes and cookies to ice cream and pastries—seemed too ordinary. There was that word again. Well, *she* might be ordinary, but she wasn't going to create an ordinary dessert! She rejected her ideas as fast as she wrote them down. If there were ever a time for making a bold, risky move cooking-wise, it was now. But she could think of nothing with real pizzazz.

Feeling frustrated, she had just decided to take a brainstorming break when her roomie walked in. Since Aglaia had slept over in Calliope's room last night and Hestia had worked in the kitchen most of the day, the two girls hadn't hung out at all since those few minutes Friday afternoon.

Aglaia flopped down onto her bed, curled up with a pillow, and closed her eyes. "Phew! I could really use a nap," she said. "Calliope and I talked so late last night, I hardly got any sleep. And ever since I got up this morning, I've been helping Hephaestus in his workshop. I'm dead."

Forcing a smile, Hestia sat on her own bed, drew up her knees, and hugged them. "So you guys had fun? You and Calliope?" She tried to make her voice sound light, even though her insides tightened into a knot of worry. She was pretty sure Calliope didn't have a roommate. Not yet, anyway. What if Aglaia decided to switch roommates and move in with this new girl, leaving Hestia all alone?

"Uh-huh. Lots of fun," Aglaia replied sleepily. Then suddenly her eyes popped open and she pushed herself up onto an elbow to face Hestia. "I am a bad roommate!" she exclaimed. "I forgot to ask about your trip to the ice sculpture contest with Pheme. How'd it go? Did she talk your ear off? Like I'm doing now?"

They both grinned.

"It was great, actually," said Hestia, relaxing some. Quickly, she told Aglaia all about the trip, the amazing sculptures, and the Gray Lady judges. She even recited what the counselors had said to her, and how she and Pheme had figured their advice meant Hestia should try to put herself out there more so others could get to know her better.

Aglaia rolled onto her back to stare at the ceiling. "So the Gray Ladies just expect you to suddenly stop being shy? Like that?" She snapped her fingers.

"I guess so," said Hestia. She unclasped her knees and brought her legs down so that her feet rested on the braided rug between their beds. "Pheme thinks I need publicity," she added. "She interviewed me for her column in *Teen Scrollazine*."

"Cool," said Aglaia. Her eyes were closed again. "When will the interview come out?"

"I'm not really sure," Hestia replied. "Soon, I think."

The two girls talked a little more about Hestia's trip, and she described her favorite Athena ice sculpture. Then she sat up straighter as a sudden flash of inspiration struck her.

A sculpture. That was it! She would sculpt her banquet dessert! Not from ice, though. From cake! Her brain began to dance with cake, frosting, and special filling ideas. Maybe, since the purpose of the banquet was to celebrate the winner of the Service to Humankind Award, she could make her dessert in the shape of a trophy!

She jumped up from her bed and began to pace around the room. Was sculpting a trophy from cake even possible? Obviously, she'd need to experiment before getting too far ahead of herself.

Hearing steady breathing, she peered over at Aglaia and saw that her roomie had fallen asleep. Would she want to be woken up so she could change into her pj's? Hestia wondered. But then she decided she should just let Aglaia sleep.

Aglaia's yellow-and-blue polka-dotted comforter was bunched up at the foot of her bed, so Hestia pulled it up and stretched it over her. There. Much better!

The next night, Hestia was exploring the trophy-cake idea in the school's kitchen when Pheme suddenly walked in.

"I've been looking all over for you," Pheme told

her. Cloud-letters puffed from her lips to hang in the air near the ceiling.

"Why? What's up?" said Hestia. She had just finished mixing up an ambrosia filling she hoped to use inside her sculpted dessert. The cake she'd baked earlier was sitting nearby on a cooling rack.

Instead of answering right away, Pheme said, "I've never actually been in this kitchen before, but I remembered you spend a lot of time here. Good thing, or I'd never have tracked you down." She looked around. Her eyes roved over the huge brick fireplace, the glass-fronted cupboards, and the clean wooden countertops before coming to rest hungrily on the contents of the bowl Hestia held.

Seeing her interest, Hestia dipped a clean spoon into the ambrosia filling and held it out for Pheme to taste.

"Mmm, yummy," the goddessgirl murmured as

she licked the filling off the spoon. Then she finally said what she'd come to say. "I turned in my *Teen Scrollazine* column about you this morning. The new issue comes out Wednesday. I'll be sure you get a copy hot off the presses."

Hestia's heart gave a flutter. "You turned in the interview already? I was hoping you might show it to me first. Is it too late?"

"'Fraid so. But don't worry. You'll love what I wrote." She grinned easily, setting her spoon in the sink. Then she began to walk around and fiddle with various kitchen gadgets.

Each time she asked "What's this?" Hestia would glance up from what she was doing to answer.

"Slotted spoon."

"Whisk."

"Peeler."

"Wow, cooking sure is a lot of work," Pheme said as she studied a pastry brush. "The things we do to set a good example for mortals, huh? Hey, maybe my interview will even boost your chances of winning the Service to Humankind Award."

Hestia shrugged. "Oh, yeah. I kind of forgot about that award. I haven't decided if I'll even enter the contest yet."

"Why not? You'd have as good a chance of winning as a lot of other students," Pheme urged. "Especially after everybody reads my article about you."

Hestia had to smile at that. Pheme was always so confident!

"But if I did put in my name, wouldn't we be, like, competitors?" Hestia asked.

Pheme shook her head. "I'm not entering. Since I'll be covering the contest for *Teen Scrollazine*, I don't think it would be right for me to be in the contest too. It'd be like a . . a . . ." As she searched for the term she was after, she waved a potato masher in the air.

"Conflict of interest?" Hestia supplied. It was a term she'd learned in Ethics-ology class last year. It meant a situation in which there were conflicting aims. In this case, Pheme probably figured she'd have a hard time writing objectively about the contestants if she were one of them.

"That's it." Pheme nodded. "Besides, I won the contest I most care about when I got hired to do my column for the 'zine." With a grin, she started for the swinging door.

"Hey!" Hestia called, gesturing toward Pheme's hand. "Tater masher?"

"Oh yeah," said Pheme with a quick laugh. "Didn't mean to be a masher-napper." She returned and stuck the masher back into the container where she'd found it. Then she headed out again.

Alone again once more, Hestia focused on her dessert experiments. However tasty her ambrosia filling was, it proved too soft to hold the pieces of chocolate cake together. In fact, her ambrosia-filled cake sculpture was starting to look more like a big-eared bear head than a trophy. It had turned out so awful, it couldn't even be the consolation prize for *last* place. It was nearly bedtime, so she might as well pack it in for tonight.

Yawning, she stashed the cake pieces and filling in the larder. Then she started for the kitchen door. When she passed the hearth, her gaze fell on the cooking pot that hung from a hook in the fireplace. Seeing the huge kettle reminded her of her symbol idea. The one her classmates had laughed at. Mr. Phintias had said that the symbol she picked should show how she'd like others to see her, so she should choose something with power and pizzazz.

If not a cooking pot for my symbol, then what? she wondered as she swung through the door and into the cafeteria. A potato masher? She giggled at the thought. Talking to Pheme had sparked her interest in the award. She didn't expect to win, but entering would be a way of putting herself forward as the Gray Ladies had advised in their one-toothed, roundabout way. The contest sign-up was tomorrow. Hmm. If she could just think of a halfway decent symbol . . .

Later that night, after Hestia had finished her homework and climbed into bed, Aglaia returned to their room. "Oh! Did I wake you? Sorry I'm so late," she murmured when Hestia rose onto her elbows.

"Nuh-uh, you didn't make me," said Hestia. "I wasn't asleep yet." Suddenly, she sniffed the air and sat up straighter. "Hey! Is that smoke I smell?"

"Yep, it's just me, a little singed around the edges," said Aglaia. "There was a bit of an explosion in the forge just now while I was helping Hephaestus with one of his projects."

"You're both okay, though?" Hestia asked in alarm.

"We're fine, which is more than I can say for my chiton." Aglaia moved over to her closet and began to change out of it. After showing Hestia what a sooty mess it was, she balled it up and lobbed it across the room into her trash can. "Score!"

"Nice shot," said Hestia, sitting all the way up in bed. "But what happened exactly?"

Aglaia shrugged on her bathrobe and then said, "The Service to Humankind committee asked Zeus to ask Hephaestus to make a trophy. It'll be presented at Saturday's banquet to whoever wins."

"Trophy?" Hestia echoed, seeing her dessert idea go down in flames.

"Yeah. We were melting metals for the trophy mold when some thingamabobber part inside the forge exploded. You should have seen the shower of sparks!"

"Ye gods!" Hestia exclaimed. "Sure you didn't get hurt?"

Her roomie nodded. "Unless you count getting covered with soot." With a wave, she headed for the door again. "I'm off to take a shower."

After Aglaia left their room, Hestia flopped onto her stomach. Back to square one. If Hephaestus was making a trophy as the award for the winner of the contest, she couldn't make a trophy-shaped dessert. It would be too much the same. She'd have to sculpt something else. Hmm. But what?

. . .

The next morning was Monday, a school day. Hestia got up extra early and put on a pale green chiton. For half a second she considered leaving its hood down. She even stepped into the hall with her head bare, but when she heard someone coming, she pulled the hood up. Maybe tomorrow was soon enough to make another change.

She hurried down to the kitchen before breakfast and chanted her spell to light the fire in the kitchen hearth. Oatmeal was on the menu today, and she'd promised Ms. Okto she'd get things started. As the wood under the huge cooking pot ignited, so did an idea in her brain. Not an idea for her dessert, but one for her symbol. Suddenly, she knew exactly what it should be! Her new idea had power. It had pizzazz. It was perfect!

"See you later!" she called to Ms. Xena, who was

just coming out of the larder with a carton of eggs. Then she hurried out the kitchen door.

After crossing through the cafeteria, Hestia pushed past the exit door and made her way down the main hall of the school. There was a crowd of students around the award sign-up sheet that had been posted on the wall near the lockers. Feeling shy, Hestia hovered nearby, trying to look busy and not draw attention to herself until everyone else had signed up and gone off to breakfast.

Alone at last, she approached the sign-up sheet, took hold of the pen attached to it, and neatly printed her name. She was just about to write her symbol idea on the blank line beside her name when she heard someone give a yelp behind her in the hall.

"Ow! Watch it!" Asca's voice yelled.

She whirled around, spotting him immediately.

He wasn't using his camouflage, so he was pretty noticeable. Especially since he was hopping around and howling.

Just beyond him stood Kydoimos and his just-as-annoying best friend, Makhai. "Sorry, lizard-dude. Accidents will happen," Kydoimos said. Laughing together, the two boys quickly disappeared down the hall.

She'd bet anything they'd stomped on Asca's tail. On purpose.

"You okay?" Hestia asked, going over to him. He was holding his tail behind his back. Because he didn't want anyone to see it was a stump? She gasped in alarm and checked the floor just in case his tail really had broken off.

"Please tell me you aren't looking for my tail down there," Asca said, gritting his teeth in pain.

"It's okay, see?" He swung it around to show her.

"So your tail doesn't really pop off if you get too startled?" Hestia asked, genuinely interested.

Asca gave a snort. "No way! No more than your head pops off when you're surprised. When it's stepped on, it's like when you bump your elbow hard. Throbs for a while. Then it's okay."

She nodded and then said, "So what Pheme wrote about your tail in her column wasn't true, I guess."

"Not at all," Asca said. He was staring at her hand for some reason. She glanced down to see that she still held the sign-up pen. She had pulled it free of the string and tack attaching it to the wall. He peered beyond her to the sign-up sheet. "Putting your name in for the award?"

"Mm-hm," Hestia admitted shyly. As she turned back toward the sign-up sheet, he stepped closer.

"I've just got to fill in the symbol space, and then I'm done," she told him.

At that moment Apollo came by. He nodded at Asca before veering off toward the cafeteria. "How's it going, Stumpster!" he called out.

Looking over at him, Asca casually called back, "Hey, god-dude."

"Doesn't that bother you?" she asked him, her hand hovering over the blank space beside her name. "That nickname, I mean?"

Asca shrugged, seeming surprised by the idea. "Not really. The guys are always giving each other nicknames. If you think about it, immortal titles are actually nicknames too. I'm the godboy of lizardry. And you're goddessgirl of the hearth, right? I remember Mr. Phintias calling you that in class."

She nodded. "Before I started at the Academy I

suggested to mortals in my village that they might want to keep a fire burning in a public hearth in each city, and they started calling me that. But your nickname—Stumpster. It's not even accurate!"

"Courtesy of Pheme, that bit of misinformation has stuck to me as tight as my tail. You can't fight it, so the best thing is to roll with it, I've decided. It's no biggie. Not to me, anyway."

Hestia wasn't sure if he was being truly honest about the nickname not hurting his feelings, but she didn't push the subject. Still, it was no wonder he'd warned her to be careful about what she said to the goddessgirl of gossip!

A shiver ran down her spine. What exactly had Pheme written about her? Was she going to get a nickname as a result? What would it be? The Cookster? Bakerrific? Recipeep? Soupergirl? She'd just have to hope for the best. Setting pen to paper, she scribbled down the symbol she'd picked—a flame!

Asca peered over her shoulder. "Cool—I mean, warm! I like your symbol." He grinned.

"Thanks," said Hestia, grinning back. She held out the pen to him. "Your turn," she said, but he shook his head.

Holding both hands palms out, he took a step backward. "Nope. I think I'll wait for a Service to Reptiles Award," he quipped. Then he eyeballed the sheet. "I was just curious to see how many students had signed up. Seems like fifty, maybe sixty? Based on some of the names here—Kydoimos's and Makhai's, for instance—I'd say your odds are pretty good of making it to the final eleven."

"Thanks," she said. "But I don't really care. I just want to, you know, put myself forward for a change."

Asca's locker was only a few down from the sign-up area, so after she reattached the pen to its string, she waited around as he headed there. He pulled a puffy green jacket from his locker and slipped it on. Seeing her look of surprise, he gave a laugh. "Lizards are cold-blooded. I never feel like I'm warm enough," he explained.

"Really? I'm the opposite—always warm enough, never cold," she told him.

"Then a flame is definitely a good choice for your symbol."

Hestia smiled shyly. Then in a burst of boldness she blurted out, "I'm actually pretty good at making flames. Want to see?" Immediately, she worried that she'd sounded boastful. "Oops. I hope I didn't just sound like that full-of-himself sculptor Pygmalion."

But Asca just laughed, not seeming even a bit put

off. "Yeah, I remember that show-off. He's always telling everyone what a great artist he is. That's bragging. You're just offering to show me your skills. Nothing wrong with that. Here, though?" He scanned the mostly-empty hall. "You won't burn the place down?"

She grinned, shaking her head. "No worries." She took a step back from him and his locker. Cupping her hands, she chanted her spell:

"Come, spark,

Light the dark.

Blaze higher,

Make a fire."

Instantly, a flame burst to life above her cupped palms. It glowed bright yellow-orange, with a hint of blue at its center. At first it was tiny, a few inches tall. But as she widened the gap between her palms, it grew till it was nearly a foot high.

"Cool! Um, I mean hot," joked Asca, looking awed. "That's totally amazing. Don't your palms get burned, though?"

She scrunched her nose a little, shaking her head. "They get a teeny bit warm, but that's all. It doesn't hurt or anything." *Clap!* She brought her hands together quickly to extinguish the flame.

Suddenly, she had a thought. When those haystack counselors had mentioned her "light," had they been hinting at the very symbol she'd chosen? The flame?

When the lyrebell sounded breakfast, they headed off to the cafeteria. Asca was easier to talk to than a lot of other people. Still Hestia could still hardly believe she was walking side by side with a boy!

They split up when some godboys called out, "Hey, Stumpster, over here! We saved you a place in line!" The wry smile Asca sent her before he went to join his friends made her decide that he really didn't mind his nickname after all.

As she picked up a tray and went to stand at the back of the line, panic started to set in as she considered her dessert for next Saturday's banquet. It was just a little over five days away. Truthfully, though, she was glad to give up on the trophy idea. The shape had turned out to be too hard to sculpt. She needed something simpler.

Deep in thought, Hestia took a plate of hambrosia and eggs and a carton of nectar once she reached the front of the line. Then she veered off into the dining area, still thinking hard. Those oddball school counselors had urged her to share her "gifts." Did they mean they thought she should tell the world about her cooking? If so, maybe the Pheme interview had been a wise move after all?

She was so busy mulling this over that she didn't

even notice when she sat at a table with two girls she didn't know. Feeling their eyes on her, she blinked at them. "Oh, sorry! Okay if I sit here?"

"No problem," one of the girls said. "Hey, didn't we just see you making a flame in your hands in the hall? What's that about?"

"You saw?" Hestia had been so intent on showing Asca her flame that she hadn't even noticed the two girls. Pleased by their interest, she was talking a blue streak to the two girls before she knew it. The girls weren't experienced cooks and seemed fascinated by everything Hestia told them. Soon they were all laughing over her story of trying to make a trophy cake that turned out to look like a bear. It was almost like she was Pheme or something!

9

Half Truths

THE CLASSROOM WENT QUIET WHEN HESTIA walked into second-period Crafts-ology two days later on Wednesday morning. She was aware of students sneaking peeks at her as she went to sit at her four-person table (as if she'd just been a topic of conversation!).

Automatically, she reached to pull her chiton's hood over her head. But since she'd forgotten she'd cut it off this particular outfit two nights before. Argh! What a dumb idea that had been! It was just that she'd felt emboldened by her friend-making success with those two girls she'd accidentally sat with at breakfast. She'd figured she still had other chitons with hoods, just in case this whole new, bolder, shine-your-light version of herself didn't work out as well as she'd hoped it would. However, that didn't help her right now.

Pandora turned in her chair and leaned over to Hestia. "Did you see Pheme's column in *Teen Scrollazine*?" At the next table, Aphrodite gestured toward the copy she was reading. It was open to an article titled "What's Cooking in the MOA Cafeteria?"

Hestia's stomach tightened nervously. "No, not yet. I knew she was going to write about me, though." Pheme had promised her an early copy, but she must've forgotten.

"Is it true that the anteater kitchen lady, Ms. Xena, is only allowed to serve meals and clean up afterward, not cook?" Pandora asked now as Aphrodite listened in. "Because she's a horrible cook and almost gave the entire MOA student body pepper poisoning once?"

"What? No!" Hestia blurted in alarm. "Did Pheme write that?"

Shooting Hestia a look of sympathy, Aphrodite leaned across the aisle and handed over her copy.

"Thanks," Hestia told her with a small smile. She began skimming the article fast, hoping Mr. Phintias wouldn't arrive and start class before she could finish reading it. Two seconds later she groaned. "Oh no! This isn't right. It's not what I told Pheme. I mean, Ms. Xena did over-pepper the yambrosia once, but that was an accident any cook could've made. And there's stuff in here about Ms. Okto that—"

"Pheme means well, and she's a good writer," interrupted Aphrodite. "But everyone knows she mixes fact with fiction. So don't worry."

"And it does make her column fun and exciting, don't you think?" said Pandora.

"But how can readers know which parts are truthful and which are exaggerations?" Hestia groaned again. "Ms. Xena and Ms. Okto are not going to be happy. I hope they don't think I actually said these things about them."

Hestia couldn't bear the thought of her cafeteria-lady friends being hurt because of her. She grabbed her schoolbag and half rose from her seat. She never skipped class, but she had to go to the kitchen. Right now!

Ping! Ping! Principal Zeus's wife, Hera, walked in just as the start-of-class lyrebell pinged. "Good morning, everyone. I will be substituting for Mr. Phintias today," she announced from the front of the room. A regal-looking goddess with thick, blond hair styled high on her head, Hera owned and ran a wedding shop called Hera's Happy Endings in the Immortal Marketplace. However, when there was a need, she also subbed at the Academy.

Hestia sank back down in her seat. Trapped. For now, anyway. She'd just have to hope Ms. Xena and Ms. Okto were too busy to bother reading the new issue of the 'zine.

"As you may have guessed," Hera told the class, "Mr. Phintias is currently at Principal Zeus's temple in Olympia. Now that the eleven finalists have been selected by the Service to Humankind Award committee, he and other artists are hard at work depicting their images in a mural."

Instantly, there was a murmur of voices. "Who are the finalists?" Pandora asked. "Can you tell us?" It was nice to have her around sometimes. Especially when she asked the very same questions you were reluctant to ask but wanted to know the answers to.

Hera smiled. "The award committee has been very hush-hush about that. But my understanding is that the finalists will be revealed when the mural is unveiled tonight." As another murmur swept over the classroom, she added, "Anyone who is interested can attend the unveiling. And I hope you all will." Then she told them they could have a free period to work on a craft of their choice or on homework for another class.

A cheer went up. Then everyone got to work. Usually, Hestia was a model student and always followed directions. But today she hid Aphrodite's *Teen*

Scrollazine atop her Hero-ology textscroll so she could read Pheme's column closely from beginning to end while appearing to read homework.

Hestia, goddessgirl of the hearth, is so shy that few people know who she is, much less that she's an expert cook. Well, that wasn't so bad, Hestia decided. She read on. *In fact, most of the items on the menu in MOA's cafeteria—from yam-brosia to celestial salad to her new rosemary-olive bread and those yummy chocolate ambrosia bars—are her invention.*

Hestia cringed. Yes, she had invented the recipes for those particular menu items, and several others. But no way was she responsible for "most" of the MOA menu. Talk about exaggeration!

As she continued reading, her dismay only increased. The article was even worse than she'd thought at first glance. *Without Hestia's culinary expertise and guidance, MOA's kitchen would not run as efficiently as it does. When*

Ms. Xena (who most students know as the "anteater" lunch lady) almost poisoned the student body with an unhealthy dose of pepper, Hestia wisely removed her from cooking duties and reassigned her to tasks more suited to her abilities, like cleaning and serving meals.

Feeling sick to her stomach, Hestia had to stop reading. Pheme had vastly overstated her talents and accomplishments at Ms. Xena's expense.

And Ms. Okto would be none too pleased if she saw the article either. She was head cook after all, and the efficiency of the kitchen was a credit to her!

Since no one had been reading the scrollazine at breakfast, copies could only have just arrived at the school, right? Maybe she could get to the kitchen before any of the cafeteria ladies saw Pheme's column. Then she could explain what she'd really said and how Pheme had twisted her words. She had to put things right!

Getting up from her table, Hestia handed the scrollazine back to Aphrodite. After mumbling a quick thanks, she made her way to the teacher's desk at the front of the room. How she wished she had never said yes to Pheme's interview! She should have stayed hidden and unknown. Life had been safer and simpler that way. The advice those dumb Gray Ladies had given her was just wrong, wrong, wrong! Zeus should fire them from doing counselor work.

"I don't feel so well," she told Hera. She really didn't, so it wasn't a lie. Her fingers gripped her schoolbag tightly. "Can I leave?"

"Oh, that's too bad," Hera said sympathetically. "You do look a bit pale. Of course you may go. Perhaps you'd better lie down in your room for a while. Or see the school nurse?"

There was a nurse at MOA? Hestia hadn't realized

that. But she didn't really need medical help. Just a place to hide.

"Thanks," she said. "I think I'll try lying down." But instead of going to her room, she hurried to the cafeteria and dashed inside. When she swung through to the kitchen, she saw that Ms. Okto and a thin, sour-faced part-time assistant named Ms. Mahlab were already starting to get things ready for lunch.

Seven of Ms. Okto's eight hands were busy slicing, dicing, and spicing the ingredients for a casserole. Before Hestia could say anything, Ms. Okto waved her one free hand in the air. "I'm so glad you're here early," she told Hestia. "Ms. Xena had to leave unexpectedly, so we're shorthanded for lunch."

"Do you know where she went?" Hestia asked anxiously. She moved to the hearth, which she'd lit before breakfast, and lifted the big iron kettle from its hook. Then she went to the sink to fill the pot with water, since she could see that Ms. Mahlab was chopping vegetables for soup.

Ms. Okto shook her head. "She left too quickly for me to find out. On an urgent errand, she said. But you know how reliable she is. I'm sure she won't be gone for long if she can help it."

Yes, Hestia did know how reliable Ms. Xena was. Yet Pheme's column had made it seem like the lunch lady was careless and incompetent! "Did she seem upset?" Hestia asked nervously.

"Would you blame her if she was?" Ms. Mahlab said with a snort. "We all read Pheme's contribution to the new *Teen Scrollazine*, and—"

"I'm so sorry!" Hestia began. "I—"

"Oh, that silly gossip column," Ms. Okto interrupted,

frowning at the assistant. "I never pay it any attention. That girl could whip up news out of thin air."

Ms. Okto was trying to be nice. Still, Hestia's heart sank when she realized she was too late to shield her friends from any pain that article caused them.

"Yes, but that story about Ms. Xena—" Ms. Mahlab started to protest.

Ms. Okto waved one of the five knives she was wielding. "Ms. Xena knows better than to pay any heed to that rag," she said quickly. Then she thrust a mop at Ms. Mahlab and told her the lunchroom floor needed cleaning. Sulkily, the assistant left the kitchen.

Since the floor had been sparkling clean as she'd come through the cafeteria, Hestia knew this was just busywork to keep Ms. Mahlab from saying anything more.

Hestia tried another couple of times to apologize about Pheme's article, but Ms. Okto brushed her words aside. "I told you, I don't pay gossip any mind, and neither should you." Finally, the two of them wound up working silently, side by side. Hestia felt horrible. Had things changed between them forever? That would make her so sad.

When lunch was ready to serve, Ms. Okto went out to dish up food with Ms. Mahlab. Hestia sat alone in the kitchen to eat. She didn't feel like subjecting herself to the curiosity of other students. Most of them would have read Pheme's column by now.

After she finished lunch, she began to mix up more cake batter, with her banquet dessert in mind. But filled with guilt and believing she was to blame for Ms. Xena's sudden disappearance, she forgot to put leavening and salt into the batter. When the cake came out of the oven at the beginning of fourth period, it was flat and inedible. She dumped it straight into the garbage.

And still Ms. Xena hadn't returned.

Hestia didn't want to go back to class. And since Hera would've notified the office that she was sick and had left partway through second period, she figured she didn't have to. So after leaving the kitchen, she escaped to her dorm room, planning to hide out there for the rest of the afternoon.

But there was really no escape. The minute she entered her room, she saw that a copy of *Teen Scrollazine* had been shoved under her door with a note attached from Pheme. *Here it is. Hot off the presses. Hope you like it!*

"Ha!" snorted Hestia. She picked up the scrollazine and unceremoniously tossed it into her trash can.

10

The Mural

Exhausted by worry, Hestia lay down on her bed and closed her eyes. She didn't intend to fall asleep, but she did. Sometime later she woke with a start. Aglaia was standing over her.

"Is school out already?" Hestia asked groggily.

Aglaia nodded. Straightening, she pushed her brown hair behind her ears. "Why weren't you at lunch or in Hero-ology class?" she said with a look of concern. "Are you sick?"

Wider awake now, Hestia pushed herself up onto her elbows. "No, I'm okay," she said, yawning. That wasn't exactly true. She was still worried about Ms. Xena and Ms. Okto, but the nap had helped to restore her spirits a little.

"Good," said Aglaia. "Because a bunch of us are going down to the contest mural unveiling at Zeus's temple in Olympia. Want to come?" She crossed over to her desk and grabbed a hairbrush from the shelf above it. Peering into the mirror on her closet door, she began to brush out her hair.

As pleased as Hestia was at the invitation, she still felt reluctant to face other students after what Pheme had written. "I'm not sure. I . . . Have you seen the new *Teen Scrollazine*?" she asked tentatively.

Aglaia whirled around and pointed her brush at Hestia. "I knew it! You're not sick at all."

"Yes, I am. I've got *Teen Scrollazine*-itis! It's a disease caused by humiliation over that article Pheme wrote." Hestia pulled the covers over her head.

She heard Aglaia cross the room and felt her roomie sit down beside her. "Hey, turtle girl, come out."

Hestia peeked out, lowering the spread so it only covered the lower half of her face up to her nose. "Do I have to?"

Aglaia sent her a look. With a sigh, Hestia uncovered her whole face.

"That article was way over-the-top," Aglaia said. "But when are Pheme's columns not? Besides, I'm almost glad about what she wrote. You're way too modest, you know? You deserve some credit for your cooking skills. Didn't the Gray Ladies advise you not to hide your light?"

Hestia whipped the covers down and sat up in bed. "Yeah, but Pheme made it seem like I was practically the head cook. I think Ms. Okto's feelings might be hurt, even though she claims she doesn't pay any attention to gossip. And what Pheme said about Ms. Xena just wasn't true!"

"So talk to them about it," said Aglaia, going over to riffle through her closet. "But later, because I'm not leaving without you," she added, a stubborn expression on her face.

Hestia laugh-groaned and tossed a pillow at her. "Yes, ma'am!" She jumped from her bed to brush her hair and change clothes. It actually felt good to be told what to do by her roommate. Aglaia wouldn't have insisted that she come unless she really did want to hang out with her. Was Calliope coming too, though? And was it awful of Hestia to hope not?

"Hey! I like your new no-hood look!" Aglaia enthused, noticing her altered chiton. "Want me to fix your hair in a new style too, now that you're not covering it?"

"Really?" Hestia touched her hair, unsure.

Aglaia grabbed her copy of *Teen Scrollazine*. "This thing has more than just Pheme's article, you know. There are some cool hairstyles with instructions in this issue." She opened the scroll to a page with the heading "Hairstyles That Bring Smiles."

As they stood before the tall mirror on one of the closet doors, Aglaia separated Hestia's hair into five small sections and braided each of them. Then she pulled all the plaits together in back and braided them together.

"Awesome!" Hestia pronounced when her roomie was finished.

"Yeah, Calliope told me at lunch that she was going to try one of the new 'zine styles today. This one, in fact," Aglaia said, pointing to a drawing that showed a girl with her hair done in a high twist.

"Oh? Is she coming tonight too?" asked Hestia as they both made to leave the room. She hoped her tone of voice didn't betray her feelings about the idea.

"Calliope? No," said Aglaia, opening the door to the hall. "She's got homework. Hey, she's trying to find a roommate, so if you think of anybody, let her know, okay?"

Hestia brightened. Apparently, her worries about Aglaia leaving her for another roommate were all in her head! *Sweet!* But just in case, she said shyly, "Well, I hope she lucks out with her roommate like I did."

Aglaia shot her a smile. "Ditto. Come on, roomie. Let's hit it!"

Farther down the hall, they passed Artemis's room. The door was open and Aphrodite was inside telling her, "No dogs. And wear your nicest chiton. We want to look our best in case we run into adoring mortals on the way to Zeus's temple."

"Yes, sir," Artemis said, giving her a mock-salute. Seeing Hestia and Aglaia out in the hall, she grinned at them.

Hestia and Aglaia laughed. "You guys coming to the mural unveiling too?" asked Aglaia. Aphrodite assured her they were. Aphrodite and Artemis had been roommates at one time, Hestia knew. But Artemis's three dogs and the mess that went with them had been a problem for Aphrodite, so now they roomed next door to each other. They were still best buds, though. Artemis even let Aphrodite use her spare closet for all her extra clothes.

Fifteen minutes later Hestia and Aglaia boarded one of the two large chariots that would be transporting students to the temple. Theirs was the school's flashiest one. Its sides were painted deep purple, and it had an enormous gold thunderbolt on the front. The other chariot was painted blue and gold—MOA's school colors.

Among the students onboard the purple chariot with them were Hephaestus; Aphrodite and her three BFFs, plus their crushes; Medusa and her crush, Dionysus; and Pandora. Hestia looked around for Pheme but didn't see her in either chariot. Then she overheard someone say that Pheme had gone ahead to interview Mr. Phintias and the other painters about their mural. Well, those painters had better be careful what they said to her, because who knew what that cloud-letter-puffing goddessgirl might write about them!

Shortly after takeoff Athena leaned over from her seat across the aisle to speak to Hestia. "I read the article. And I like that you've invented so many recipes that make use of my olive. Just wanted to say thanks."

"Sure. I mean, you're welcome," Hestia replied. "Thank you for inventing it. Olives have so many uses, and it has such great flavor."

"Yeah, *ahlove* them," joked Heracles, who was sitting by Athena.

Overhearing, Ares, the godboy of war, turned to smile over his shoulder at Hestia. He and Aphrodite were sitting just one seat ahead. "I don't like to cook," he admitted. "But I'm really good at the eating part.

So if you ever need a taste tester, I'm your guy."

Those students sitting close enough to hear him all laughed. Hestia got several more offers for taste testing, including one from Aphrodite.

Looping her golden hair behind her ears, Aphrodite smiled at Hestia. "I know Pheme exaggerated some things. Still, I'm glad for her article. You've always been so quiet, but now we know you're far from ordinary. You're a goddessgirl of mega-talent!

Hestia beamed. "Thank you." It was absolutely the nicest thing the goddessgirl could have said to her, especially after commenting only days ago that an ordinary cooking pot fit her personality. Still, she made a point of correcting the exaggerations and errors in Pheme's article. "I only thought up *some of* the dishes on the menu, and I learned everything I know about cooking from Ms. Okto and Ms. Xena."

"Who?" asked Ares.

Hestia described the lunch ladies for anyone who didn't know their names. She was surprised and pleased when more and more students wanted to talk with her about food prep techniques and recipes. Most had at least one favorite dish they wished they knew how to make.

Her natural shyness melted away as she talked knowledgeably and enthusiastically about her favorite subject, cooking! As she was answering a question from Persephone about bread making, their chariot and the blue-and-gold one both arrived at the limestone temple in Olympia. It seemed to her that the trip had flown by, and not just because the chariots were winged!

The students climbed the steps to the most famous of all the temples in Greece, just as Mr. Phintias and the other artists were leaving. Hestia glanced up at the magnificent temple. She counted six columns across its front. There was probably double that number on each of its sides, she thought. And each column was nearly five times as tall as Zeus himself!

She glimpsed Asca up ahead of her, walking with a couple of his godboy pals. He hadn't been aboard her chariot, so he must have come on the blue-and-gold one.

Then Hestia stopped cold. Pheme was interviewing one of the painters on the temple steps! Catching Hestia's eye, she smiled cheerfully and gave her a thumbs-up. Like she had no clue anything was wrong with what she'd done.

Though Hestia returned the smile, hers was a little wobbly. She sped up, not giving Pheme the chance to speak. The ill will she'd felt toward gossipy girl had softened during the ride over, but she wasn't ready to forgive her.

"Hey, wait up!" someone called to her a few seconds later. It was Antheia, the goddessgirl of flowering wreaths, who was also Iris's BFF. Hestia waited for her on the steps.

"Just wanted to ask you to let Iris and me know when you decide on a date to start your cooking classes, okay?" Antheia told her breathlessly once she'd caught up. The cute wreath of ferns and berries that encircled her straight brown hair like a crown had slipped sideways as she'd run. She straightened it as they both continued up the steps, adding, "Pheme told us about the classes, and we want to sign up."

Sounded like Pheme was spreading more misinformation! Hestia had never said a word about teaching other students to cook. "Wasn't that a great article Pheme wrote about you?" Antheia went on. "She shared some of her ideas with Iris and me while she was writing it. She worked really hard to get it just right. I could tell she wanted you to like it."

Hearing this, Hestia felt a bit of her ill will toward Pheme dribble away, like water down a sink. She knew Pheme probably hadn't meant any harm. In that girl's mind she had only been helping. Though Hestia might wish she had gone about it a little differently, Pheme was . . . after all, Pheme. Accuracy was not her strong point. No changing that!

"It was . . . nice of her to write it," she told Antheia. "And nice of you and Iris to help her. Thanks."

"Well, let me know about the classes," Antheia said when Iris called to her from up ahead. "I want to learn to cook with some of the edible flowers I make into wreaths—put the flowers into muffins and stuff like that!"

"Oh, but . . . ," Hestia began, intending to tell her that Pheme had made a mistake about the classes. However, Antheia was already racing off.

When Hestia entered the temple a few minutes later, the first thing to catch her eye was the golden statue of Zeus seated on a throne at one end. It was hard to miss. It was huge. In fact, it was one of the Seven Wonders of the World!

She scanned the room, noting the large, ornate vases that sat in each corner. Part of the side wall was covered with a red silk curtain that she decided probably veiled the mural. Once the temple had filled with onlookers, a lady with gray hair, styled about a foot high on her head like whipped cream on a fancy dessert, stepped in front of the curtain.

She called for quiet and then addressed the crowd. "As head of the committee for the first annual Service to Humankind Award contest, it is my pleasure to reveal the eleven finalists tonight! All are Mount Olympus Academy students this committee has selected from a sign-up sheet posted in the Academy hall in recent days," she continued, building suspense. "It is from among these eleven that mortals will vote to choose one—and only one—for top honors. Voting will begin at sunrise on Friday and end at sunset."

The woman stepped toward the red silk curtain. "The masterpiece depicting the finalists that I am about to unveil will remain on this temple wall to be admired by mortals for an eternity to come! So, with no further ado—" She grabbed the edge of the curtain and swept it back.

A gasp of wonder went up from the crowd as they gazed upon the mural. Hestia craned her neck, but she could only see the very tops of the painted heads on it from where she stood. Too many people were blocking her view. Was that Aphrodite? And Athena? She couldn't exactly tell.

But suddenly those around her were congratulating her and pushing her forward toward the mural. Soon she was standing right in front of it.

Colorful images of the eleven contest finalists ranged across the wall, each one shown with the student's chosen symbol. Their names were carefully inscribed at the base of the painted figures. And guess what? Her likeness and name were part of the mural. She was a finalist! The crowd oohed and aahed over the magnificent painting and gave a cheer for the group of eleven. Each was asked to pose before their image so an artist from the *Greekly Weekly News* could draw them.

Hestia could scarcely believe that she was a finalist! Not only that—she was right smack in the middle of the group! Her painted likeness was the only one that faced completely forward. The five figures on either side of her angled toward her, as if drawn to the flame she held, which seemed to cast its light over the entire group of eleven students. Aphrodite's image (holding a heart-shaped mirror) stood directly next to hers, and Athena's image (with an owl perched on her shoulder) was on Hestia's other side.

The other eight finalists included Iris, with a rainbow over her head; Persephone, with a bouquet of flowers clutched to her chest; Pandora, holding a box with a question mark on its lid; Poseidon, with his trident at his side; Ares, gripping a spear; Dionysus, with a grapevine threaded in his hair; Heracles, wielding a knobby club; and Apollo, strumming a lyre.

The mural artists had given Hestia's image a sweet expression that also looked . . . well . . . *confident*. Not meek at all! While she'd never thought of herself as confident before, she hoped with all her heart that it was really possible she could become that goddessgirl in the mural. She was trying to!

"Squee!" Aphrodite exclaimed to Athena after the artist had finished his drawings for the *Greekly Weekly News*.

"Hugs!" Athena replied, giving her BFF a congratulatory one. Then the two goddessgirls turned to all the other finalists and hugged them too, Hestia included.

"Love your flame symbol," Aphrodite told her. "As Mr. Phintias would say, it's got pizzazz. Suits you way better than a cooking pot."

A warm feeling filled Hestia at her words.

"Congrats, roomie!" Aglaia squealed, running up to hug her.

"Yeah, props!" Asca said, coming over too. He was wearing his green jacket again. "And you got the center spot. Awesome!"

"Thanks," Hestia told them. After Aphrodite and Aglaia were called away by other friends, she darted a look at Asca. "Did you see Pheme's article?"

"I wasn't going to bring it up unless you did," he said. Then he teased her. "I never realized you ran the whole MOA kitchen operation. Wow! With such a heavy responsibility it's amazing you can still find time to attend classes."

Hestia gave him a mock-punch on the arm. Joking back, she said, "Yeah, it's a tough job. But I do my best. I just hope I don't wind up with a nickname."

"Hmm. What nickname goes with a flame?" said Asca, tapping a finger on his chin. "I know. Sparky!"

Hestia ducked her face into both hands, laughing. "Oh, please. Nooo!"

When the students filed out of the temple to board chariots for the ride back to MOA, a group of earth-bound mortals came up to them. Hestia started to step aside, assuming they'd come to see Aphrodite to ask her advice about love problems, as they so often did. To Hestia's surprise, however, some of them headed her way.

"Will you autograph my *Teen Scrollazine*?" several of them asked her. They held out their copies, open to Pheme's column.

Bemused, Hestia shook her head. "Oh! Really? I'm sorry, but I didn't bring a—"

But before she could finish, Aphrodite, who had

overheard, smiled and whipped out a pink feather pen. "You can return it later." With a casual wave, she went off to join her friends already in the chariot.

As Hestia signed her name in pink on one 'zine after another, one of her fans gushed admiringly, "Your public hearths have been such a gift to the towns and homes around here!"

"Yeah," said a man as several others nodded. "With a ready source of fire, we never have to worry anymore that we won't be able to cook food for our families. Or that we won't be able to create a fire for warmth when we need it. It was such an obvious idea. I can't believe no one else ever thought of it before."

"That's why immortals are so amazing," gushed another fan. "Always helping us solve problems, big and small. Thank you!"

"I don't suppose you'd consider sharing some of

your recipes with us, would you?" a young woman with a heart-shaped face and long black hair asked. "The dishes Pheme mentioned in her article about you sound so delicious!"

Hestia had barely drawn breath to answer when Pheme fluttered up. "You're not the only one asking!" the spiky-haired girl breathlessly told the group of fans. "Since my column came out this morning, *Teen Scrollazine*'s office has been flooded with requests for Hestia's recipes!"

Hestia drew back her head. "Really?"

"So how about printing them in each issue? It could be a new column!" the young woman with the long black hair suggested. "You could call it Hestia's Home-Cooking." At this, a cheer went up from the group of mortals.

"That's an awesome idea," Hestia said, her eyes

shining with excitement. But then she glanced uncertainly at Pheme. "What do you think?" she asked. After all, none of this would have been happening if it hadn't been for Pheme. Hestia wouldn't want the gossipy girl to feel like she was stepping on her toes by starting her own column with *Teen Scrollazine*.

But Pheme seemed totally on board with the idea. "Are you kidding? You're my discovery. The 'zine editors are thrilled with me for finding you. And I know they'll adore the idea, if you're willing and have time."

"I'll make time!" said Hestia. "I love writing recipes. I probably already have enough to fill columns for an entire year."

As they waved good-bye to the adoring mortals around them and made their way to where the chariots were parked, Hestia reached over and bumped Pheme's arm with hers. "Thanks," she said. "For noticing me and for . . . everything." She'd finally forgiven Pheme the errors in her article and really meant it. In a way, Pheme had done her a favor.

Pheme smiled back. "Anytime. Well, gotta go. See you back at school!" With that, her small orange wings began to flap, and she was zooming off, in a hurry as usual.

On the way back to MOA, Hestia marveled that a day that had started out so badly could have turned out so well. The only thing that could make it better was if she could square things with Ms. Okto and Ms. Xena. It was cool to make new friends, but not if it meant she had to lose the ones she already had!

11

Cleaning Up

SINCE IT WAS NEARING THE END OF DINNERTIME, the students from the chariots were all starving when they finally got back to Mount Olympus Academy. The cafeteria was pretty full by then, the din of clattering dishes and chattering kids a dull roar. But when Hestia and the other students entered, a cheer went up for the award finalists.

How did they know? wondered Hestia. Then she

noticed Pheme flitting around the room. Aha! So that's why Pheme had been in such a hurry earlier. The cloud-letters floating above her head showed that she was spreading the word about the mural. News always traveled fast when that orange-haired goddessgirl was around!

Ms. Okto was in her usual dinnertime spot, handing out plates of food at the head of the line, but Hestia didn't see Ms. Xena anywhere. Deciding to fortify herself with food before checking for her in the kitchen, Hestia grabbed a tray and got in line.

Argh! She wound up behind Kydoimos and Makhai again. Did they know about the mural? Probably, with Pheme around.

Seeing her, the two boys nudged each other. "Hey, it's Flame Brain, Queen of the Kitchen," Makhai quipped, squinting at her. Kydoimos laughed in a mean way.

Hestia felt herself pale. She'd never been a target of these boys' teasing before, but the interview—and maybe the mural in the temple too—seemed to have changed all that. Automatically, she shrank away from the two meanies, reaching to pull her hood over her head. But as her hand pawed the air, she remembered again that the chiton she was wearing was hoodless now.

Suddenly, her sweet but confident mural image flashed through her mind. *Why not try to embody that image?* she thought. Drawing herself up, she looked from one boy to the other. "Actually, my nickname's Sparky," she told them. Flipping her hair over one shoulder the way she'd seen Aphrodite do, she added, "And I prefer 'empress' to 'queen.'"

They gawked at her, appearing dumbfounded that meek little her was standing up to them. Taking courage, she smiled sweetly. "Also, you might be interested to know that I'm working on a new lunch meat recipe, and I've decided to name it after you two." She paused. "It'll be called bully-oney."

A few students nearby overheard and snickered, but Kydoimos and Makhai didn't seem to have a comeback for once. Instead, they grabbed two of the eight plates of food that Ms. Okto was holding out to the next eight students in line, and slunk away.

It popped into Hestia's mind that by not letting Kydoimos and Makhai get the better of her, she'd accomplished one of her two remaining goals. She'd stood up for someone—herself! Check!

Just one last thing on her recipe card list to accomplish. She reached into her pocket for the card, but realized it was in her other chiton. No biggie. She remembered what she'd written: *Take a truly big, bold*

cooking risk. Well, that was something she hoped to do with her dessert for Saturday's banquet. If only a big, bold, risky idea would come to her!

Ms. Okto was grinning as she handed Hestia a plate. Because the cook had overheard what she'd said to the bullies, or because she was pleased to see her? Maybe the latter, since she said, "Word has it you made the finalist list. Congratulations, sweetie pie!"

"Thanks," said Hestia. "Everything okay?"

Ms. Okto nodded. "Ms. Xena's back, thank goodness." Then she added, "Sorry about being in a bad mood earlier. I assure you it had nothing to do with Pheme's column. Chef Soterides has been a thorn in my side all day. That man could annoy the skin right off a potato!"

When Hestia laughed, Ms. Okto did too. Then the

lunch lady returned to dishing up food and handing it out to the next bunch of kids.

Buoyed up by Ms. Okto's cheerfulness, Hestia changed her mind about sitting down to eat in the cafeteria. Instead, she took her plate and headed for the kitchen to see if Ms. Xena was there.

She was! Hestia found her sucking up a nectaroni noodle that had fallen onto the kitchen floor. After setting her tray on the closest countertop, Hestia grabbed a dishcloth and began to wipe up a splatter of sauce she'd spotted nearby.

"What are you doing?" Ms. Xena scolded. "That's my job. Cleaning is suited to my abilities, as you may have heard."

Hestia winced. The phrase had come straight out of Pheme's column. "I'm so sorry," she said earnestly. "Pheme got a lot of things wrong in that column she wrote. And she left out the most important, nice stuff I told her about you. Like how you're the kindest, most generous, most wonderful person ever. And how you've taught me so many things. And how you rescued me from loneliness when I first came to MOA!"

"Hey, where's all this coming from?" Ms. Xena asked in surprise. She stopped vacuuming to lean against the counter.

Hestia straightened. "Aren't you mad? About the column?"

"No! Of course not! Everybody knows how Pheme is. It was obvious to me you hadn't said most of that stuff. I took her words with a grain of salt. Or rather, pepper."

At that, a laugh burst from Hestia. Ms. Xena grinned. "Actually, I kind of like all the attention I've been getting since that column came out. All I have to do now to get kids to jump to it and obey the cafeteria rules is to pick up a pepper shaker like I mean business!"

"I'm so relieved!" said Hestia. "When you weren't around at lunch, I thought maybe you were mad at me over the column. Where'd you go, anyway?" She scooped up a forkful of nectaroni from her plate and took a bite. Mmm! Delish!

Ms. Xena gave her a sideways look as she bent her head to suck up another stray noodle she'd found on the floor. Then she actually blushed! "I thought Ms. Okto might've told you. No? Well, I guess *I* will, then. I'm leaving the Academy at the end of next week."

"What? Why?" Hestia straightened again, suddenly losing interest in her dinner.

"I went for a job interview today. And I got it! I'll

be working under Chef Soterides in a new restaurant in the Immortal Marketplace. It'll be called King Nikomedes' Fish and Fowl."

Ms. Xena looked so thrilled that Hestia couldn't bear to burst her bubble. "I'm happy for you!" she managed to say. But really, she felt totally lost. She depended on Ms. Xena like a second mom. And now she was leaving?

"And I heard your good news, too," Ms. Xena said now. "Congratulations on making finalist in the Service to Humankind Award!" She gave Hestia a big hug.

"Thanks," said Hestia. She glanced around the kitchen. "Can I help you with anything?" No way could she eat any more dinner. There was too big a lump in her throat because of Ms. Xena's news.

To stop herself from tearing up, she grabbed a

dish towel and began to dry some newly washed pots and pans in the countertop rack. While Ms. Xena continued to clean up spilled food, Hestia described the mural in the temple and her surprise and pleasure at getting the center spot.

"So you are pretty much queen of the mural?" asked Ms. Xena.

Reminded of the nickname Kydoimos and Makhai had tried to pin on her, Hestia made a face.

"What?" asked Ms. Xena. That was all it took to prompt Hestia to spill the beans about what had happened in the cafeteria line.

"Bully-oney?" Ms. Xena doubled over with laughter. But then she grew thoughtful. "I know those two can act mean sometimes, but deep down I'm sure they're good boys."

Hestia considered this. "Maybe deep, deep, deep

down. As deep as the Underworld, that is!"

They both laughed again. Afterward, Hestia gave Ms. Xena a hug. "You're the best," she told her. "And I love that you always see the good in everyone. I'm going to miss you, though. Who am I going to tell all my life stuff to after you're gone?"

"To your new friends! Don't think I haven't noticed all the ones you've been making this week. And I'll only be a short winged-sandal flight away, you know. Come visit me at the IM anytime," Ms. Xena told her. "I'll be disappointed if you don't!"

By the time Hestia left the kitchen a while later, she felt a tiny bit better than she had at first about Ms. Xena leaving MOA. At least she wouldn't be too far away. And that lady was way excited about her new adventure. So Hestia would try to truly be happy for her as well.

On Thursday, Hestia continued her dessert experiments in third period and during her free time. And on Friday morning, remembering Ares' half-joking remark about his willingness to serve as a taste tester, she felt emboldened to ask around for volunteers to do just that. She needed as much help as she could find to get things right before the banquet!

By the end of classes she had five recruits total, including Ares. The other volunteers were Aphrodite, Asca, Aglaia, and Hephaestus. She didn't tell them they'd be taste testing the dessert she was creating for the award banquet, however.

As soon as her last class of the day ended, Hestia hit the kitchen to mix up the first of three test cakes and pop it into the oven. She was still planning to make some kind of cake dessert, though she hadn't yet decided on what shape it would take now that she'd abandoned the trophy idea. By the time her recruits arrived, cake number one was cooling on the counter. Unfortunately, she'd accidentally taken it out of the oven too soon.

Ares was the first to sample a bite of the under-baked cake. "Mmm, this chocolate pudding is epic," he declared.

More like an epic fail, thought Hestia, gazing at the slumping gooey mixture. Aphrodite elbowed Ares in the side, sending Hestia a quick apologetic look at the same time.

"Ow!" Ares protested. "What did you do that for?"

"It's okay," Hestia told them quickly. "I want everyone's honest feedback." Glancing at Ares, she said, "I'm glad you like it. Only thing is, that was supposed to be a cake, not pudding."

"Oh, sorry." Ares ducked his head sheepishly. Then he perked up again, waving his spoon. "But who cares. It's good!"

"Yeah!" Asca grinned as he licked the spoonful he'd scooped up.

"On to taste test number two," Hestia announced. While mixing up the batter for her second attempt, she cracked an egg with one hand.

"Hey, that was awesome!" said Asca.

"There's a trick to it," she told him. She placed a whole egg in the palm of her hand. "You have to strike it on the edge of the bowl with just enough force so that it cracks in the middle, and then you ease the cracked shell apart with your index and middle finger." She demonstrated as she spoke. "Voilà!" she said as the goop inside her egg dropped neatly into the bowl.

They seemed so interested that she continued the

lessons while her second cake baked in the oven. She got a couple dozen more eggs from the larder and passed them and some small bowls around so the others could practice.

"You made it look so easy, but . . ." Aglaia gave hers a whack. She stared in dismay when her egg yolk broke on her first try and pieces of shell landed in the bowl.

The same thing happened to Aphrodite when she tried. The two girls fished out the shell bits with a spoon, which took some time because the pieces kept sliding back into the bowl.

"At least your eggs landed in the bowl," Hephaestus said. His had totally missed and glopped onto the counter.

"You'll get the hang of it. It takes a lot of eggs-perience to become an eggs-pert," Hestia joked. The others laughed. And suddenly, everyone was cracking puns as well as eggs.

"I hope there won't be an eggs-am on this later, or I'll flunk for sure," Asca said. He'd given his first egg such a hard knock that it had smashed.

Only Ares got the hang of one-handed egg cracking right away. "Eggs-cellent!" he crowed when his very first egg cracked down the middle and fell neatly into his bowl with the yolk intact.

"Beginner's luck," huffed Hephaestus.

"I bet you can't do it twice in a row," Asca challenged.

But Ares did. "You want to hold the egg kind of like you're throwing a curveball," he counseled the others.

"Duh, I've never thrown a curveball in my life," Aphrodite protested. "This is eggs-asperating!"

Nevertheless, after several more tries, almost everyone managed at least one success.

Before taking her second cake out of the oven, Hestia checked it carefully. "I think this one's more done. You can tell because it's shrunk a little from the edges of the pan." Reaching inside the oven she pressed down lightly on the top of the cake. "It feels firm, too—another good sign."

"Mmm, that smells sooo good," said Aglaia as Hestia finally moved the cake from the oven to the counter.

"Can we try some?" asked Ares eagerly.

Aphrodite gave his reaching arm a light tap with her spoon. "Not unless you want to burn your fingers and your mouth!"

While waiting for this second cake to cool enough to cut, Hestia let the others help mix up the ingredients for a third cake. Most of them didn't know how to measure and sift. But that made sense, she realized. Till now they'd had little opportunity to cook.

"I guess I never thought about how our food gets prepared and winds up on the table," said Ares as Hestia slid her third cake into the oven. "It's just always there."

Splat! They looked over to see that Aglaia had accidentally knocked an egg onto the floor, where it had exploded. She and Hephaestus began cleaning up the mess. "Explosions seem to be our thing lately," Hephaestus joked. Then he and Aglaia told the others about their near disaster earlier that week when something in the forge had exploded and shot out flames.

Hmm, thought Hestia as she set a bowl into the sink to be washed later. *Explosions.*

And suddenly she went still. Because a fabulous new dessert idea had just come to her. The one she'd been searching for!

Would her idea be too showy, though? Too dangerous? But then she recalled what the Gray Ladies had said to her at the ice sculpting contest: "When you hide your light under a cooking pot, you deprive others of your gifts. And you also cheat yourself."

The others kept talking, but now Hestia was only half listening. Hephaestus was leaning against the counter, absently twirling his beautiful silver cane and saying something about the Service to Humankind Award. "I heard the line for the voting was so long, it snaked down the steps of the temple and up the street."

"I bet the vote counting will take all night," Asca put in.

"Think cake two is cool enough to taste test yet?" asked Ares. Like Zeus, he had a one-track brain when food—particularly anything sweet—was being offered.

"Huh?" Hestia came out of her dessert-inspiration daze and touched the top of the cake sitting on the counter. "Definitely," she announced. She sliced off samples and handed them around.

Ares practically inhaled his piece. "Whoa! Dis is duh bes ake iver ha," he mumbled with his mouth full.

Aphrodite froze, her fork half-raised to her lips. "The best cake you've ever had?" She frowned at him. "Better than the birthday cake I spent hours putting together for your last birthday party, even?" she challenged.

Ares blinked. "Wha— No! I mean—" Looking uncomfortable, he pulled at the neck of his tunic.

Uh-oh, thought Hestia. She didn't want her cooking to cause any trouble between these two!

But then Aphrodite tasted the cake. "Oh, wow," she said, her blue eyes widening in pleasure. "This is mega-yum. And so light and fluffy!" A small smile played around her lips as she said to Hestia, "Maybe you could teach Ares how to make a cake like this for my next birthday!"

With a relieved smile, Ares said, "Sure! I'm halfway there since I've already mastered egg-cracking-ology!"

"Seriously, though, we should have a class or something," Aglaia told her. "I bet others around here would like to learn to cook too."

"Maybe," Hestia replied lightly. Antheia and Pheme had said something along the same lines. So why not really do it? The more she thought about the possibility, the more excited she got. Ms. Okto would probably let her use the kitchen after the final dinner cleanup once a week. That way, cooking students wouldn't be in the way of regular meal preparations. It was worth an ask.

After the recruits also tested cake number three—which was almost but not quite as delicious as cake two, everyone decided—they cleaned up. All volunteered to help with the cooking and setup for the banquet the next day.

It seemed to Hestia that she was finally crawling out of her turtle shell. Ms. Xena was right. She did have new friends. And if her cooking class became a reality, it would be sure to result in even more new friendships. A win-win!

12

The Banquet

HESTIA ZIPPED INTO THE KITCHEN BRIGHT AND early on Saturday morning. She could hardly wait to try her dessert idea. It was going to be a time crunch, though. The banquet was tonight!

First off, she mixed enough chocolate cake batter to fill three round cake pans of graduated sizes, using the recipe her recruits had favored. The pans ranged in diameter from nine inches to eleven inches to thirteen inches across. While the layers were baking, she mixed up sugar cookie dough, dyed it green, and cut it into three-inch-tall tree shapes. Then after the pans of cake were out of the oven, she put the cookies in to bake.

When the cake layers had cooled, she used a nectar-flavored icing between the layers to "glue" them together, stacking the layers from largest to smallest, so that they formed a tiered, mountainlike shape. Next she put the large three-layer cake into the larder to keep till later.

That done, she made a quick trip to the Supernatural Market, where she bought ambrosia ice cream. All part of her plan to wow the banquet-goers. If her dessert was a disaster, she'd be letting Ms. Okto down. Still, it was a risk she was determined to take, and one that would fulfill the final goal on her recipe card list. It just *had* to work!

Later that morning her friends arrived to help out with the main meal preparations. They gathered round Ms. Okto while she demonstrated how to slice and dice vegetables using a rocking motion from the tip of the knife to the end of the blade. "If you keep the fingertips of the hand not using the knife curled so that only the flat part of the knuckles face the blade, you'll be less likely to cut yourself," she told them.

While they cut veggies to be used for celestial salad and other side dishes for the banquet, Aphrodite, Ares, and other friends they had recruited were over in the open-air domed cupola at the top of the Academy. There, they were seeing to the decorations and setting the tables. The cupola was quite large for a cupola, but Hestia figured it would probably prove just big enough to accommodate all the finalists and guests tonight.

Meanwhile, in the kitchen, Ms. Okto began making the main dish that she and Chef Soterides had finally agreed upon—a special nectar-glazed roast lamb. It would be accompanied by a pot of rice seasoned with a blend of spices that Hestia had come up with.

Hestia was pleased to see that her friends were getting to know and appreciate the cafeteria ladies the way she did. When a piece of carrot Aglaia tried dicing fell to the floor, she, Hephaestus, and Asca barely flinched when Ms. Xena used her snout to suck it up.

Eventually, all was done and Ms. Okto shooed Hestia out to get all dressed up in her finery. Happily, Aglaia, Hephaestus, and Asca had volunteered to work as servers during the banquet, so Hestia would see them again.

She could feel herself getting anxious as she headed for the dorm to change clothes for the banquet. Not about the contest. About her dessert! The finishing touches couldn't go on it till the very last minute. Not until the banquet was nearly over, in fact. Which was the sort of drama that was going to make her way more nervous than finding out who won the award!

When Hestia entered her room, she gasped at the sight that met her eyes. There was a beautiful sparkly gold chiton lying on her bed! A note beside it from Aphrodite read: *Thought you might like to borrow this for tonight. Gold's not really my color, but I think it will look fabulous on you.*

How nice of her! thought Hestia. This was the kind of thing friends did for one another. She did a little happy dance. She had friends now!

Quickly, she slipped the chiton on and then checked herself in the closet door mirror. Aphrodite was right, she decided. The chiton did look fabulous on her, if she did say so herself. It brought out the gold flecks in her brown eyes and the glints of gold in her brown hair that were usually invisible. Nevertheless, she did feel a bit flashy as she ventured out of her room in the sparkly chiton. Was this outfit really her?

Risk it, she told herself. She was so done with being invisible. And this sparkly dress was the opposite of that, for sure. Besides, she had more important things to worry about than what she was wearing. Namely, her dessert!

She arrived at the top of the MOA cupola's winding staircase just as the other ten finalists were being led from there into the banquet room. Quickly, she joined the end of the line. Her eyes widened with pleasure as they entered the cupola. Tables had been set in arching rows facing a stage, and were filled with people there to celebrate. Special guests, teachers, contest committee members, and Principal Zeus and Hera, all stood to honor the finalists as they filed in.

"Everything's so cute!" she heard one of the finalists ahead of her murmur. It was true. Aphrodite, Ares, and their friends had done an amazing job of decorating. Gold and silver streamers, possibly left over from Ares' recent birthday party, were wound around the tall columns that encircled the inside of the domed cupola.

And floating in the air, held up by a magic spell, were symbols representing the eleven finalists. There was a cute toy club and a toy spear (for Heracles and Ares), a prism that broke the light into rainbows (Iris, of course), and a red heart-shaped pillow (for Aphrodite). Hestia's flame symbol was represented by a beautiful, lit scented candle in a holder that resembled cupped hands.

The linen-draped finalists' table was long and elegantly set with the Academy's best plates, rimmed with gold. It was up front, and their seats were lined up on one side of it so that they sat facing the rest of the room. Name cards showed where everyone was to sit. Hestia was in the middle, with Aphrodite and Athena on either side of her. They'd all been placed in the same order as they'd been portrayed in the mural!

She picked up the card next to her plate. Her name was written on it in beautiful swirly, swoopy calligraphy. She ran her thumb over the letters, and they magically recited her name: "Hestia." She giggled. Overhearing, the other finalists did the same with their cards.

Hestia leaned over to Aphrodite. "Thanks for letting me borrow this outfit."

"Anytime," said Aphrodite. She was wearing a

stunning rose-colored chiton with a ruffled hem. "I knew gold would look great on you."

"It really was nice of you. Pink may be your favorite color, but I think you've got a heart of gold," Hestia quipped.

"And you're as sweet as those chocolate cakes you baked last night, to say so!" They both laughed.

Once everyone in the room sat down again, dinner was served. All went perfectly, though Asca tripped over his own tail when he brought in the platter of roast lamb. Everyone gasped in horror as the roast sailed into the air, but somehow he managed to do a dive and maneuver the platter under it as it came down. *Plop!* The roast landed with only a minimum of splattered juices.

"Good catch!" Apollo called out. "Ever thought about playing javelin ball? We could use you on the team!"

227

Asca grinned. "Sure! I bet balls wouldn't be any harder to catch on the tip of a javelin than a lamb roast is to catch on a platter."

The banquet-goers all laughed. Hestia smiled at Asca when he served her a slice of the nectar-glazed lamb. "Tail okay?" she asked.

"Still attached if that's what you mean," he said with a grin.

Hestia grinned back. "Good thing Pheme isn't sitting near enough to hear you say that." The goddessgirl of gossip was attending the banquet as a special guest so that she could write about it for *Teen Scrollazine.*

"Yeah," Asca agreed. "It'd be all over her next column!" After a moment's hesitation he added, "You look like a winner tonight. I mean, I hope you win tonight." Then his cheeks flushed bright red.

"Hurry up with that platter!" Ares called from farther down the table. "I'm so hungry, I could eat Heracles' club!"

"Hey!" said Heracles, overhearing. He shot Ares a fake look of alarm and wrapped both arms around his club as if to protect it. Which cracked up all the finalists.

"Thanks," Hestia told Asca before he moved on to serve the others. She wasn't entirely sure, but she thought maybe he'd been trying to say she looked pretty. No boy had ever told her that before. Maybe he'd never said it to a girl before either, which was why he'd gotten so flustered. It was kind of nice!

When everyone had eaten and the dishes were being cleared away, Hestia started to get nervous again. She slipped off to the kitchen to finish making her dessert.

Seeing her, Ms. Xena smiled wide with approval. "How pretty you are!"

"Yeah, gold's a good color for you," Ms. Okto added.

"Thanks," said Hestia with a quick grin. "Ready?"

With the ladies' help, she set the large three-layer chocolate cake she'd baked on a silver tray and placed that on a fancy wheeled cart. Then they began the last-minute prep. This was the tricky part!

Hestia piled ambrosia ice cream on top of the cake in the shape of an overturned bowl, which made her "mountain" even higher. At the same time, Ms. Okto beat several egg whites and a handful of sugar to make a stiff white meringue. Working together, they completely covered the cake and ice cream with the meringue.

Now, her dessert resembled a snow-covered

mountain. It was Mount Olympus in winter! She scooped out enough space at the very top of her snow-covered mountain to hold half an eggshell that she was going to add later on.

Her hands shook a little as she moved her flame around to carefully brown the egg-white meringue. She'd been afraid she'd accidentally burn it. Or that the flame might melt the ice cream that was piled on top of the chocolate cake base. That would have caused her creation to collapse! Fortunately, however, her cake mountain stayed upright and the meringue browned evenly to a pale gold that matched her chiton. Perfection!

While Mrs. Okto made a quick trip to the cupola to check on things, Hestia placed the half eggshell she'd saved from the eggs she'd cracked (with one hand!) into the space she'd made for it at the very top of her creation. She filled the bowl of the eggshell with a special golden liquid that Ms. Xena had saved for her to use.

The lunch lady helped Hestia place the tree-shaped cookies she'd made earlier all around the base of her chocolate cake mountain. "Fantastic. It looks like a forest below a snow-covered mountain," Ms. Xena praised.

"Fingers crossed that it tastes fantastic too," said Hestia.

"You'd better get back to the cupola lickety-split," Ms. Okto told Hestia, pushing through the kitchen door just then. All eight of her hands were balancing stacks of dishes she'd cleared from the cupola. "Hera just told me that the head of the contest committee is going to make her announcement before dessert is served."

Sensing Hestia's reluctance to leave her dessert behind, Ms. Xena helped to shoo Hestia off. "Scoot. We'll carry this mountain up in just a minute. It'll make a big splash."

"Thanks!" Hestia was suddenly glad she didn't have to bring in the dessert herself. Nervous about how everyone would like her creation, she might accidentally do an Asca, but really drop it!

Back in the cupola she slid into her seat at the finalists' table just as Zeus was finishing a speech. "And now the moment we've all been waiting for," he roared, his blue eyes twinkling. He glanced toward Hades, who was sitting at a drum set in a corner of the room. On cue the godboy of the Underworld played a drumroll—*brrum, brrum, brrum, brrum.*

The head of the contest committee stood up beside Zeus, a letterscroll clutched in her hand. *Brrap-a-*

tap-tap! Hades finished up. A sense of expectation swept the room.

The committee head bowed to Zeus. "Thank you for that most kind introduction," she said. "And for sponsoring this banquet to honor some of Mount Olympus Academy's finest and most generous students."

Her eyes scanned the table of finalists. "Every one of you has done worthy things to benefit humankind," she told them. "And I want you to know that yesterday's vote count was very close."

Hestia was not completely surprised to hear this. When she thought of all the things the students sharing her table had collectively done for mortals down on Earth, she felt proud to be a finalist. She hoped that all of them had gotten at least some votes.

The head of the committee paused to slip a blue

ribbon from the cream-colored letterscroll she was holding. Hestia wished the woman would hurry. If the contest winner wasn't announced soon, the meringue-covered ice cream at the top of her dessert would surely melt!

It seemed to take forever as the gray-haired woman shook the letterscroll to unroll it, then studied what was written on it. Hestia peered worriedly at the cupola door.

The committee lady looked back up and smiled. "And the winner of the first ever Service to Humankind Award is . . ." Drawing out the suspense, her eyes roamed from contestant to contestant.

Despite herself, Hestia found her heart suddenly beating wildly. What if there really was a chance that she'd won?

But then the committee head boomed, "Athena!"

Hestia felt a brief surge of disappointment. She wondered if the other finalists did too. Athena had won many contests already. Including the Temple Games a short time ago. But with her clever inventions and her wisdom and all that, Athena really had done more for humankind than anyone else at their table. This was an award she truly deserved.

Recovering quickly, Hestia turned toward Athena and joined in the cheers and applause that followed the announcement.

The committee head gestured for Athena to come up beside her to accept the fabulous golden trophy that Hephaestus had crafted with Aglaia's help. Zeus was beaming at his daughter, his blue eyes full of delight. He was obviously proud of her, and who could blame him?

Athena accepted her trophy and spoke a few

words of thanks, sounding surprised and pleased. That was one of the truly nice things about her, thought Hestia. She never bragged or acted like she even realized how great she was!

As Athena took her seat, there were new murmurs of excitement as Ms. Okto and Ms. Xena arrived, bearing the banquet dessert. Hestia jumped up from the table and went to help. The ambrosia ice cream at the top was still frozen. Her mountain wasn't going to collapse. Hooray!

"Do I spy dessert?" Zeus roared happily. Sparks of electricity flew from his fingertips as he eagerly rubbed his palms together, but they quickly fizzled out as he patted the empty area atop of the table in front of him. "Set it here," he commanded.

One did not disobey the King of the Gods and Ruler of the Heavens if one knew what was good for one, so that was exactly where Ms. Okto and Ms. Xena placed it.

After positioning herself to one side so as not to block anyone's view of her dessert, Hestia chanted her flame spell. Then she flicked her fingers toward the half eggshell at the top of her meringue mountain. Instantly, the amber liquid inside the eggshell blazed to life. As she spread her arms wider and wider, the bright yellow-orange sparks that sizzled upward grew into a fountain of sparks shooting half-dozen feet high!

"Magnificent!" yelled Chef Soterides, who was seated at the same table as Zeus and Hera. Ms. Okto beamed at this. *Phew!* Hestia hadn't let her down.

"It's a volcano!" someone shouted from the side of the room as the dessert continued to sparkle high into the air.

"No, it's Mount Olympus!" shouted someone else.

"Let's eat!" boomed Zeus.

At this, clapping and cheering filled the room. Once the fireworks died down, Ms. Xena stepped forward and handed Hestia a knife to cut the dessert. "Well done," she whispered. "I'm so proud of you."

"Thanks," Hestia whispered back. She knew she had a wide smile on her face. So much for the fifth thing on her recipe card. *Risk, schmisk!* She'd done it. Check!

Asca, Aglaia, and the other students brought in stacks of silver plates and then passed around slices of the fabulous dessert as fast as Hestia could cut them. As contest winner, Athena was given the very first slice. "Dee-licious!" she pronounced after taking her first bite.

Zeus and Hera got the next two pieces, and Zeus

dug in immediately. "Godsamighty, this is good!" he boomed, dropping crumbs on his tunic in his haste to devour his slice.

Other comments of approval circulated throughout the room. "It's fantastic!" "Scrumptious!" "Divine!"

"What's it called?" Hera asked as she discreetly handed Zeus a napkin.

Called? For a moment Hestia panicked. She'd always named her creations, but this one had been so last minute that she hadn't thought to. Mentally, she reviewed the main ingredients that made up the dessert: chocolate cake, meringue, nectar-flavored icing, and ambrosia ice cream. And for effect, flames. Then suddenly it came to her.

"Flambrosia," she announced quietly.

"Huh?" someone said. "What's it called? What did she say?"

Speaking up loudly and proudly this time, Hestia repeated herself. "It's called flambrosia!"

Hera nodded with pleasure. "The perfect name for the perfect dessert." She paused, a forkful of flambrosia halfway to her lips. "I don't suppose you'd share the recipe? I might like to make it myself sometime."

To which Zeus responded wholeheartedly, "Great idea, sugarplum!"

"I'd be happy to share it," Hestia told them. Overhearing, others began to clamor for the recipe too.

Then Pheme piped up, "The recipe for flambrosia will appear in the very first Hestia's Home-Cooking column in *Teen Scrollazine*. Watch for it in next week's issue!" The words floated high into the air in cloud-letters, letting everyone know at once.

As cheers greeted Pheme's news, Hestia caught

the spiky-haired girl's eye from across the room and mouthed the word "thanks." Even if she wasn't as shy as she once had been, having a publicity person like Pheme to get the word out was a huge help!

Afterward, everybody's forks got busy again. When all had been served—and Principal Zeus had had seconds—Hestia cut a slice of flambrosia for herself. What an amazing week it had been, she thought as she carried her plate to the finalists' table and took her seat. Not only had she been a finalist in the Service to Humankind Award and found out how much her public hearths were appreciated by mortals down on Earth, but she'd also accomplished all five of the tasks she'd set for herself, and made a bunch of new friends.

And she would soon be teaching a cooking class and sharing recipes in *Teen Scrollazine*. Ms. Okto had agreed to the class as long as the students cleaned up after themselves. Hestia would miss Ms. Xena a ton, but if that lunch lady wanted to pursue a new challenge, then good for her. In fact, Hestia could hardly wait to check out the new restaurant Ms. Xena would be working at in the IM!

Aglaia had offered to help make a poster tomorrow to advertise the new cooking class. They would put it up in the locker area, along with a sign-up sheet, and see what happened. Maybe there were other undiscovered cooking talents at MOA. Regardless, anyone could benefit from knowing the basics of cooking. Like how to crack an egg.

Even after Ms. Xena left, Hestia would continue to let her light shine, just as the Gray Ladies had advised. Yes, there were risks—she could fail, embarrass herself, and so on—but playing it safe was also risky, especially when she considered how many good experiences she might miss. Life was a dish to be tasted!

Speaking of which . . . Hestia picked up her fork and took a bite of flambrosia. Then closing her eyes, she savored the sweet flavors. Mmm.

Don't miss the next adventure in
the Goddess Girls series!

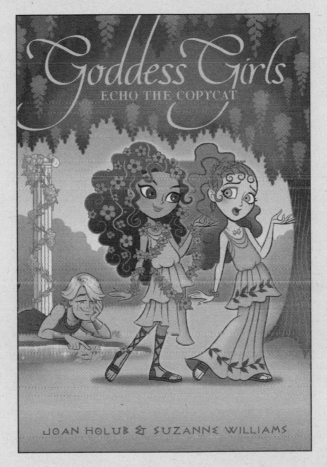

Coming Soon